Gabriel raised his head, the glitter in his eyes making her pulse race even faster.

Taking her other hand too, he drew her inexorably closer, until their bodies lightly touched, his thighs against hers, her breasts brushing his shirt.

'Rhiannon?' His breath stirred tendrils of hair at her forehead.

Her eyes felt heavy-lidded but she made herself look at him. She raised her eyes to his, and saw herself reflected in the dark centres.

'Rhiannon,' he said again, 'would you like me to kiss you?'

Alarm flared and died. She was suddenly very calm and sure. His mouth was close to hers, its contours beautiful in a wholly masculine way, firm but not narrow, decisive yet promising tenderness.

Scarcely above a whisper, against the thunder that was the sound of her racing heart, she said, 'Yes.'

D0756397

Daphne Clair lives in subtropical New Zealand, with her Dutch-born husband. They have five children. At eight years old she embarked on her first novel, about taming a tiger. This epic never reached a publisher, but metamorphosed male tigers still prowl the pages of her romances, of which she has written over thirty for Harlequin Mills & Boon®, and over fifty all told. Her other writing includes non-fiction, poetry and short stories, and she has won literary prizes in New Zealand and America.

Readers are invited to visit Daphne Clair's website at www.daphneclair.com.

Recent titles by the same author:

CLAIMING HIS BRIDE
THE MARRIAGE DEBT
THE RICCIONI PREGNANCY

THE DETERMINED VIRGIN

BY
DAPHNE CLAIR

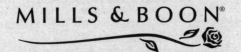

MILLS & BOON®

First published in Great Britain 2003
Harlequin Mills & Boon Limited,
Eton House, 18-24 Paradise Road, Richmond, Surrey TW9 1SR

© Daphne Clair 2003

ISBN 0 263 83319 4

Set in Times Roman 10½ on 12½ pt.
01-0903-43044

Printed and bound in Spain
by Litografía Rosés, S.A., Barcelona

CHAPTER ONE

RHIANNON hated elevators, but the parking building's lower floors had already been full when she'd driven in this morning, and carrying a box of ceramic tiles up four-and-a-half flights of stairs wasn't sensible. Any normal person would take the easier option offered by the invitingly open doors.

She'd spent five years trying to be a normal person.

Taking a deep breath, she stepped inside and pressed the button for level four, relieved she was the only passenger.

As the doors were about to meet, a strong masculine hand parted them and a tall, grey-suited man stepped through the gap. Rhiannon quickly moved back, her spine coming up against the far wall.

The newcomer glanced at the lit number on the keypad and the doors slid together.

It's all right, she told herself. *He's just an ordinary man.* Needing reassurance of that, she sent a covert glance at him, and discovered with a shock that, leaning against a side wall with his arms folded, he was giving her a lazily interested inspection, lids half-lowered over silvery eyes that roamed from her chin-length, dark brown hair to her cream shirt and moss-green skirt.

Rhiannon's nape prickled, every tiny hair standing on end, and her heartbeat increased. She tried to breathe steadily, remain calm. But even as she tightened her grip on the box in her arms and concentrated her gaze on the changing numbers over the doors, her brain registered that her companion didn't look ordinary.

The suit, and the blue-striped shirt worn with a dark silk tie were conventional enough, perfectly fitted to a lean body that seemed to arrange itself naturally to his casual stance. But his face belonged on some ancient statue in a sunlit Grecian setting—not half a world away in the rather dingy surroundings of a parking building in downtown Auckland. Thick, almost-blond, sun-streaked hair added to the impression, its incipient waves tamed by a conventional but expensive-looking haircut.

Number two came up on the display, then three, four. The man let Rhiannon out first, following as the doors whooshed shut behind them. She hoisted her box a little higher and quickly headed for the half-flight of concrete steps leading to 4-B.

As she reached them he touched her arm. 'That looks heavy,' he said. 'Let me help you.'

Her foot, already on the first step, slipped as she instinctively pulled away, turning her head to refuse the offer. She lost her balance, falling onto the stairs, and her elbow hit a concrete edge, the box slid from her grasp.

Tiles spilled, smashing against each other. Dizzy with pain, she scarcely heard the explosive word the man let out before she twisted upright on one of the steps and sat nursing her elbow, teeth gritted and eyes squeezed shut to stop herself crying out.

'I'm *sorry!*' The deep male voice was very near, and her eyes flew wide, to see the Greek-god face only inches from hers, the man hunkered down before her,

one knee on the not-too-clean concrete floor. 'I didn't
mean to startle you,' he said.

Close up, his eyes were blue—ice-blue but not cold,
and filled with guilty concern. 'Are you hurt?' He looked
at the hand cupped about her throbbing elbow. 'Let me
see?' His bent head came even closer, so she could see
the parting among the glossy waves of his hair. A pleas-
ant, slightly astringent aroma hinting of citrus and spicy
manuka leaves came to her.

He extended a hand to touch her again, and Rhiannon
instinctively shrank back, shaking her head. 'It'll be
okay in a minute.'

'You're pale,' he said abruptly.

Not surprising; she felt pale. But the dizziness was
wearing off. 'I'm all right.' To prove it she tried to lever
herself up.

'Don't move!' A large hand reached out to hold hers
against the cold concrete. 'You'd better stay there a
while,' he said. And as she resisted his hold, 'Take it
easy.'

She didn't know if the last remark was a continuation
of the first, or a reaction to her attempt at escape. But
his soothing yet authoritative tone helped to still her
panic.

This man is not attacking you.

Making an effort to relax, she realised that the hand
imprisoning hers was warm and, to her surprise, almost
comforting. Then he took it away, and began picking up
the tiles and replacing them in the box.

'Some are broken,' he said. 'I'll replace them, or pay
whatever it costs you.'

'You needn't,' she told him. 'I was going to break them up anyway.'

About to place two jagged pieces in the box, he gave her a smiling glance of inquiry. 'Stress relief?'

'They're for a mosaic,' she explained reluctantly. Talking might help relieve the throbbing ache at her elbow. 'Most of them are already damaged.'

'Mosaic…a hobby, or do you do it for a living?'

Rhiannon hesitated. *It's just an idle question, don't be silly.* 'Not entirely.'

'Would I know your name?'

'I doubt it.'

When she didn't volunteer it, he sent her another glance, his sculpted lips taking on a slightly wry curve, then closed the flaps on the carton and asked, 'How are you feeling?'

'I'm fine.' She adjusted the strap of her shoulder-bag, starting to rise again, and winced.

The man frowned. 'Are you sure you haven't broken a bone?'

Rhiannon moved her forearm, testing. It was uncomfortable but she said, 'I'll have a bruise, that's all.' Carrying the tiles would be a problem, though.

He said, 'You go first—I'll bring this along for you.'

With no real choice, she mounted the steps, conscious of his footsteps behind her.

When he'd stowed the box in the back of her station wagon he asked, 'Anything else I can do for you?'

'No. Thank you, you've done enough.'

'Ow!' he said softly.

'I didn't mean…'

He laughed, and Rhiannon said quickly, 'It was kind of you and I appreciate it.'

'That's generous, since I caused you to get hurt.'

'No, it wasn't your fault.' Considering his spectacular good looks, any other woman would surely have gracefully accepted his initial offer of help. Instead of falling over her feet in an effort to get away.

'Is there someone to help you unload them?' he asked her, indicating the tiles.

'Yes.' Not giving any more information, she opened the driver's door and climbed in.

His expression rueful, he closed the door for her, raised a casual hand and stepped back.

Glancing in the rear-vision mirror as she entered the ramp to the lower level, she saw he was still watching.

As the station wagon disappeared down the ramp, Gabriel Hudson shoved his hands into his pockets and rocked briefly on his heels.

Nice one, Hudson. Not up to your usual style.

Not that he was in the habit of picking up females in car parks, but he'd seldom been brushed off so unequivocally. Even before he'd bought out a failing business for a song, changed its name and built it up to the rank of one of New Zealand's top private companies, he'd been spoiled for choice as far as female companionship was concerned. His looks were both an asset and an occasional embarrassment. They didn't usually scare women off.

The instant he'd stepped into the lift this one had scurried into a corner without making eye contact, allowing him to study her for a moment or two before she looked up and caught him.

She'd seemed startled then—large green eyes, slightly almond-shaped but enormous and wary as a cat's, fixed on him for a long second, unpainted lips parting on a quickly indrawn breath. Tempting lips—their outlines very feminine and well-defined, the tender flesh blush-pink.

Shining mahogany hair cut in a deceptively simple style kissed petal-smooth skin with a faint dusky-rose bloom that had disappeared alarmingly into a deathly pallor when she hurt herself. The box she'd carried had partly hidden her figure, but her plain skirt had been just short enough to reveal nicely shaped legs.

She'd looked away again immediately, the soft lips firmly pressing together, and he'd seen the taut line of her throat ripple as she swallowed, her eyes fixing on the lighted floor numbers as if she could will them to change faster.

He'd felt a throb of desire, surprising himself with the adolescent reaction to a passing stranger. His impulse to help carry the heavy box wasn't entirely altruistic. He hadn't planned seduction on the staircase, but he'd had an odd reluctance to just let her walk away. That single glance in the elevator had intrigued him.

He shouldn't have touched her. That was what had made her jump like a startled fawn and trip on the stair.

Remembering her white face, the green eyes darkened with shock, the lovely mouth pale and tight, he swore under his breath.

He'd blown his chances there, for sure. Making a

woman almost pass out with pain wasn't exactly calculated to endear a man to her.

After that there had been little he could do but see her safely to her car and forget about the disastrous encounter.

Rhiannon drove carefully, aware that her rapidly stiffening arm wouldn't stand too much strain. Her shoulder muscles were tense, and when a traffic light stopped the car she snatched the chance to practise a deep-breathing exercise, and deliberately loosened her grip on the steering wheel, flexing her fingers.

Curling them again about the vinyl, she had a clear memory of the stranger's hand on hers, strong yet not threatening. And of his eyes, that seemed to change disconcertingly from glittering silver-grey to the blue of a winter morning sky, promising warmth to come. When she'd first caught him looking at her they'd been idly appreciative, then apologetic and concerned, but later uncomfortably curious and perceptive.

The lights changed and she put her foot down, charging across the intersection before she thought to ease back on the accelerator.

She was...unsettled. On edge. A strange fluttering sensation attacked her midriff, and at her throat a pulse beat erratically. She felt warm all over and oddly weakened.

The fall, of course, had shaken her up. It would take a little while to get over it.

At the old villa in Mount Albert that she shared with another young woman, she removed a few tiles at a time from the box and carried them to the high-ceilinged former bedroom she'd converted to a home studio.

In future she'd be able to do some of her smaller artwork at her new gallery in the heart of the city, but her current commission was for a fairly large triptych. The mesh backing was laid out on the bare wooden floor, the design already partly filled in.

After stowing the tiles, she inspected her elbow and pressed a cold compress to the obvious swelling. Later her housemate, a nurse in a private hospital, insisted on prodding the arm gently and moving it about. 'Nothing broken, probably,' Janette agreed cheerfully, 'but maybe you should get it checked out.'

Rhiannon shook her head. 'If it doesn't get better,' she promised.

After dinner she wrapped the tiles in newspaper and smashed them with a hammer, left-handed, quelling a familiar inner pang at the destruction. As she'd told the stranger in the car park, most of them were already damaged, scavenged with permission from the demolition team knocking down a city building.

Fitting some of the pieces into the triptych, she soon found regret disappearing in the satisfaction of creation.

The following Friday she was entering the ground floor of the parking building when a man's deep, leisurely voice sent a tingle of recognition up her spine. The Greek god.

'Hello again.' Catching up with her, he slanted her a smile. 'How's the arm?' He looked down at it, revealed by the short-sleeved, easy-fitting beige cotton dress she wore.

'All right, thanks,' she answered warily, before remembering to return the smile.

'You still have a bruise.' It had passed the worst stage but a purple shadow remained. A long masculine finger briefly brushed the faint mark, making her flinch as a curious sensation feathered over her skin.

'Sorry!' he said, surprised grey-blue eyes meeting hers. 'Is it that tender?'

'No.' Rhiannon shied sideways, creating a space between them as he walked beside her.

He sent her a quizzical look. 'Then—I apologise for taking liberties.'

'It's all right,' she said coolly. Such a fleeting, scarcely felt touch couldn't be construed as an assault, or even an advance of any kind. Many people touched casually, naturally, with no suggestion of intimacy.

She headed for the stairs, and he commented, 'Not taking the lift?'

Rhiannon shook her head. Rather than admit to a phobia, she gave her usual excuse. 'Climbing stairs helps to keep me fit.'

He swerved to accompany her. 'It obviously works.' He cast a glinting glance over her.

Every nerve screamed. Rhiannon looked away and didn't answer.

'Another apology?' he inquired softly, climbing at her side.

She shook her head, her throat locked, even though her brain told her she was being ridiculous. Here was an attractive man, letting her know he was attracted to her. Most women would be pleased. Most women would have smiled at him, preened a little, even given him some kind of subtle invitation.

Rhiannon was achingly conscious that she wasn't most women.

After a second he said, 'I feel I owe you some sort of compensation. Could I buy you a coffee sometime? Or dinner?'

'You don't owe me anything,' she said tightly.

'Are you married?' he asked. 'Or in a relationship?'

The blunt question startled her into speaking without thought. 'No!'

'You just hate the sight of me? Well, I can't blame you after that accident.'

'I don't hate you—I don't even know you.'

He said lightly, 'If you'd care to…'

About to tell him she didn't, Rhiannon hesitated. If she was ever to be a normal, functioning woman she had to start acting like one. It was past time.

They had reached a landing and somehow he stopped so that he blocked her further progress though there was at least half a metre of space between them. He pulled a card from his pocket and held it out to her. 'Gabriel Hudson,' he said. 'I'm in the air-freight business.'

A name to be reckoned with. Gabriel Hudson owned one of the biggest and best-known private firms in the country.

The card confirmed it—the familiar angel-wings logo in one corner, his name centred in flowing script. All the company's ads used the theme of care and speed, featuring angels cradling precious parcels gently in their arms as they flew from one end of New Zealand to the other, and around the globe. Their service was popular because, unlike most such companies, they boasted a door-to-door service, every package remaining in the Angelair system from collection to delivery.

He was a respected businessman, widely admired for his commercial success when still in his twenties, and named last year on the modest national rich-list, but not one of those who were photographed living it up at social occasions attended by the local glitterati. His private life, it seemed, was strictly kept that way—private.

'I've used your service,' Rhiannon blurted. Who hadn't used Angelair if they were involved in any kind of business in New Zealand?

'We carry your mosaics?'

Feeling a need to cover her gauche remark, she said, 'Other people's art, too, and books.'

'Books?'

'I have a gallery and bookshop.'

His head tilted to one side. 'Where?'

She'd said too much already. Reluctantly, she told him, 'We moved a few weeks ago into High Street.' The lease for the new premises was cheap for central Auckland, though twice what she'd paid for a small suburban shop space. She hoped the extra street trade and a change to more exclusive stock would compensate.

'What's it called?'

Pointless to hold back now. 'Mosaica.'

A young man came bounding up the stairs, and Gabriel Hudson's firm hand on Rhiannon's waist moved her aside as the man raced past them with a careless 'Thanks.'

Her shoulder came up against hard male muscle, her hip just touching Gabriel's, and she recognised the citrus-and-spice scent she'd noticed at their first encounter.

Even as her skin began to prickle, her throat tighten, he moved away and allowed her to continue hurrying up the stairs.

Reaching the next floor, she paused to let two vehicles sweep past. The elevator disgorged several passengers. Gabriel said, 'Are you going to tell me your name?'

'Rhiannon,' she said, conquering long-formed habit. 'Rhiannon Lewis.'

'Ree-annon,' he repeated, as if trying out the syllables on his tongue. 'Welsh, isn't it?'

'Originally.'

'I'd like to see the gallery sometime, and maybe we could go out for that coffee?' His tone was casual, the winter-morning gaze holding mild inquiry.

This was a civilised man, a well-known, respected man, and surely so good-looking and successful that if she turned him down he wouldn't have to search very far to find some more amenable female. He'd probably write her off without a second thought. Still she demurred. 'I don't like leaving my assistant alone for long.'

'After work?' he suggested.

'I have to cash up.'

Gabriel's head tipped slightly to one side and his eyelids lowered, his mouth quirking downward.

He thought she was being coy. Remembering her earlier resolution, Rhiannon said quickly, 'That takes about twenty to thirty minutes. We close at six—except on Saturday it's at two o'clock.'

Had she really said that? Tacitly accepted an invitation from a man? Her heart plunged, then righted itself.

Gabriel nodded, absorbing the information.

He walked her to her car, Rhiannon tongue-tied now and amazed at herself. He didn't touch her but waited while she got in and fastened her seat belt. Then he closed the door, stepped back, and raised a hand in farewell as she drove off.

Heading for the stairs and his own car, Gabriel wore a preoccupied frown. After their first encounter he'd told himself the woman in the car park haunted him because he felt guilty about her fall. But when he spotted her again today he'd felt a quick leap of excitement, then a weird sensation of tightness attacked his chest, and his palms had dampened. He hadn't felt that way since the first time he asked a girl out, when he'd been a gawky adolescent. Until today.

He'd wanted to grab her, make sure she stayed at his side until he knew all about her. But, he recalled, pressing the remote button on his key ring as he approached his car, at the first touch of his hand she'd skittered away.

The sight of the name on his card had thawed her a little. Cynicism intervened for a moment, reminding him of other women who had showed increased interest when they learned who he was. But even then Rhiannon had hesitated, so that her subsequent capitulation had surprised him.

He got into the Audi and started the engine. Rhiannon. He liked the flowing syllables of her name, just as he'd liked the look of her from when he'd first seen her.

Checking his mirrors, he backed out of the space, then headed for the down ramp. So she didn't know him, but was that reason enough for her to be so unforthcoming? Was she like that with all men? What would make a woman that cautious?

A couple of things came to mind, and unconsciously his fingers tightened about the wheel. His jaw ached and he realised he had clenched his teeth hard. Consciously he eased taut muscles, telling himself not to jump to conclusions. Just because a woman hadn't thrown herself into his arms at first glance, and seemed unaffected by the curse and blessing of his face, it didn't mean there was something wrong with her.

Maybe that was what intrigued him about Rhiannon. She hadn't reacted as most women did, even though he'd frankly shown his interest, without—he hoped—being crass about it. Her cursory glances held no answering spark of awareness. And she didn't like him touching her.

That was something he intended to change.

CHAPTER TWO

GABRIEL planned his strategy carefully. It was two weeks before he strolled into Mosaica not long before closing time.

Rhiannon was at the counter serving a customer, and there was no sign of the assistant she'd mentioned.

He inspected the paintings, sculptures and other art, paying particular attention to several mosaics, and ran his gaze over the bookshelves lining the back wall, while eavesdropping on the conversation at the counter.

Rhiannon's voice was warm and confident, describing the process of firing and glazing the ceramic piece the customer had chosen, and offering gift-wrapping and postage. When she'd closed the transaction, her thanks and farewell were pleasantly friendly.

A young girl and her mother who had been browsing among the displays left seconds later. Gabriel picked out a volume on traditional Pacific carving and took it to the counter.

Rhiannon blinked when she recognised him, her face tautening infinitesimally. Not the reaction he would have preferred, but at least it indicated he had some effect on her.

Giving her his most reassuring smile, he placed the book on the counter and pulled out a credit card.

She seemed uncertain then, maybe wondering if he'd forgotten her.

No way, he told her silently. She was even lovelier than he'd remembered. And she'd been teasing his memory powerfully since their last meeting.

She entered the transaction, wrapped the book with deft movements and handed it to him. Gabriel resisted the temptation to brush his fingers against hers as he took it.

'Thanks, Rhiannon.' He noted the slight widening of her eyes before he indicated a wall-hung mosaic depicting a long-legged pukeko with shining blue plumage stalking beside a watercourse edged with reeds and ferns. 'Your work?'

She shook her head. 'Not that one.'

'The abstract designs around the doorway?' He'd been able to pinpoint the location of the gallery easily by the colourful whirls and swirls that invited customers in.

'Mine,' she confirmed.

'I'm impressed.' Small talk, designed to put her at ease, but true all the same. He released her from his gaze and glanced about them. 'It's a classy place.'

'Thank you. I hope you enjoy the book.'

'I'm sure I will. Can you spare time for that cup of coffee later?' He smiled again, a practised smile that made him despise himself.

Rhiannon hesitated, then she said in a little rush, 'You'll have to wait while I cash up.'

'No problem.' He shrugged. 'Shall I help you lock the doors?'

She looked a bit disconcerted. 'I'll do it when I leave.'

Was she afraid of being locked in with him? Gabriel didn't know whether to be insulted, appalled or amused.

She did swing the big glass door shut and turn a sign

on it to 'Closed.' Then she cleared the cash register and before disappearing into a back room, said, 'Feel free to look around some more.'

Making it clear he wasn't invited into the inner sanctum. What secrets could she have in there?

Gabriel used the time to inspect some of the gallery's wares more closely, lingering at a large, abstract mosaic panel propped against a wall.

Coloured stones, metallic paint and twisted copper wire added richness and texture to apparent randomness, clashing colours and broken lines. But like some kind of optical illusion, the colours and lines gradually resolved into intricate, mesmerising patterns.

When Rhiannon joined him at last, a bag swinging from her shoulder and a light jacket over her arm, he said abruptly, 'I want that panel. It's your work, isn't it?'

'You saw the signature?'

He hadn't but now he noticed the initials unobtrusively scribbled in a lower corner, on a piece of tile.

Not wanting to spook her, he thought better of confessing that he'd guessed, inexplicably certain that he was right. Instead he just smiled and shrugged as if she'd caught him out trying to be clever.

'Are you serious?' she asked him.

'Very serious.'

He was intrigued anew by the emotional play in her face—doubt, uncertainty, totally at odds with her manner to her previous customers.

'I'll pick it up another time,' he said, 'but I can pay now if you like.'

'That's all right. I'll put a Sold sticker on it,' she promised finally. 'And if you change your mind—'

'I don't change my mind once I see something I want.' He looked straight into her eyes and saw a flicker of alarm.

Back off, he warned himself. *This one's different.* He tried another smile. 'Shall we go, then?'

'Um…yes.'

Gabriel nodded. 'Do you need that?' He reached out, ready to take the jacket she held.

'No,' she said quickly. 'I don't think so.'

It was a warm summer evening. But he wondered if she'd have let him put it on her even if she were freezing.

What was he getting into here?

Rhiannon flicked the automatic lock and watched Gabriel pull the door closed behind them. The street lamps made his hair gleam almost bronze, the fairer streaks turning to gold.

Across the narrow thoroughfare, music with a deep, insistent beat blasted from a darkened bar. Gabriel glanced at the neon sign above and said, 'I'd like to find someplace quieter, if that's okay.'

Rhiannon nodded jerkily. 'Not too small.'

His look was mildly questioning, and she said, 'I like a bit of room to move, don't you?' He was a big man; surely he'd want to be able to stretch those long legs.

'I know what you mean,' he conceded easily. 'Those cubbyholes where two pairs of knees won't fit under the table and you have to take care not to accidentally bump your neighbour with your elbow aren't very comfortable.'

They walked side by side, Gabriel with one hand in his pocket, pushing back the edge of his jacket, the other swinging loosely at his side. Tonight his suit was dark, and he had no tie. The opened collar of his shirt showed a glimpse of lightly tanned skin.

A young couple heading in the opposite direction, arms about each other and oblivious to other pedestrians, almost ran into Rhiannon. Gabriel's firm touch on her waist steered her out of the way, then he dropped his hand.

After turning at the next corner, he paused at a lighted doorway. 'How does this look?'

Through the glass doors Rhiannon saw a spacious room with people at cloth-covered tables under glittering but muted chandeliers.

'Expensive,' she said.

He laughed and pushed open one of the doors. 'I can stand it. Will it do?'

'Yes,' Rhiannon agreed hastily and stepped inside.

They were ushered to a table and Gabriel asked, 'Would you like a real drink?'

She shook her head. 'Just coffee, thanks. I'll be driving later.' Besides, she wasn't sure she could cope with drinking and this man as well.

'Have you eaten?'

'Yes.' She'd had a take-away salad earlier in the evening, bolting it down between customers.

'What about a dessert? I could do with one myself.' He asked the waitress for dessert menus, and looked over the top of his at Rhiannon. 'I can recommend the chocolate-cherry gateau, but the crème brûlée is good too if you want something lighter.'

She hadn't been sure she wanted anything at all but, glancing the menu, she found her mouth watering.

'Do you come here regularly?' That was a safe topic.

'Now and then. It's handy to my office and the service is usually quick.'

Which implied that he didn't often have time to spare—or didn't like wasting it. Well, she didn't suppose he'd got where he was by sitting around eating desserts and drinking coffee. 'I'll try the crème brûlée,' she decided.

Gabriel opted for the gateau, and ordered their coffee. Then he laid his arms on the table and said, 'Tell me about yourself.'

Rhiannon looked down and untwined the hands tightly wrapped about each other in her lap. 'The gallery is my bread and butter, and I do mosaics when I have the time.'

'Do you take commissions?'

'Sometimes. Mostly I do my artwork at home and sell from the gallery.'

'Where would that be…your home?'

She shot a wary glance at him. 'Mount Albert.'

Gabriel leaned back in his chair. 'So, are you an Aucklander born and bred?'

It sounded like an idle question, mere chitchat. Rhiannon shook her head. 'I was born and bred in Pukekohe.'

'A country girl?' he quizzed.

'Not really. We weren't into market gardening.' That was what the rich red volcanic soil in the area was known for. Making an effort to relax, she added, 'My father had an electrical service business.'

'Had?'

She waited a moment. 'He's in a nursing home now. He was involved in a motorway accident, along with my mother.'

'And your mother?' Gabriel asked quietly, his eyes darkening in sympathy.

'She died. My father has some brain damage. He needs twenty-four hour care.' A familiar sadness touched her, for the man her father had once been.

'That must be difficult for you, as well as for him.' Gabriel paused, searching her face. 'When did it happen?'

'Nearly six years ago.' She looked down at the table-cloth, and it blurred before her eyes. 'I've had time to get over it.' If a person ever did get over these things.

He laid one arm on the table, forefinger idly tracing a circle on the cloth before he looked up again. 'Did you have family to help?'

'My grandmother.' Without her, Rhiannon didn't know how she would have survived that horrible year. 'She was wonderful.'

'I'm glad. You were very young to be bereaved like that. Do you have brothers or sisters?'

Rhiannon shook her head. 'Do you…?'

'A younger brother who works for me, heading the Australian office, and a sister in the States. My parents are divorced but they both live in New Zealand with new partners.'

It was common enough and he didn't sound particularly traumatised. 'How old were you?' she asked.

'Ten.'

At ten he would have been vulnerable. She wondered how long it had taken him to get over his parents' split.

'Now,' he said, 'I'm thirty-two.'

Carefully she offered, 'I'm twenty-three.'

He made a rueful face. 'I was hoping you were older.'

She should laugh, but instead she looked away again, fiddling with a spoon on the table. 'I feel older.'

'Why is that?'

Studying the distorted reflection of the room, she answered, 'I've been running a business since I was in my teens.'

'Early ambition?'

'Not really.' Seeing he was waiting for more, she explained. 'After the accident and…and my mother's death, my grandmother decided to retire from her business and put me in charge.' It had meant giving up her university studies, and sometimes she regretted that, but the offer had been a lifeline. She'd been too traumatised to concentrate on study and exams, and since her father couldn't work and she'd used the money from the sale of his business to care for his needs, she'd had to earn a living.

'Your grandmother ran a gallery?' Gabriel guessed.

'A suburban handcraft shop in Onehunga. Needlework, ceramics, a few paintings and carvings. I sold my first mosaics there after I took it over. The gallery evolved over time, and people began coming to it from all over the city.' Rhiannon halted to steady her voice, replacing the spoon on the tablecloth. 'I inherited the business when my grandmother died.'

Gabriel cast her a quick glance. 'When?'

'Almost three years ago.' The cancer that killed her had been mercifully quick, but her death had left a huge hole in Rhiannon's life.

'Tough,' he commented. Perhaps guessing she didn't want to talk about that, he said, 'Opening in High Street's a bold move.'

'It's a risk, but I did my homework. I'm ready to move on.'

He gave her a thoughtful look. 'You're not given to taking risks lightly, are you?' he said slowly.

How could he know, on such a brief acquaintance? Her neck stiffened warningly. 'I like to know where I'm going.'

'Sometimes it's fun to take a step in the dark. You never know what it might lead to.'

His eyes had turned silver again, in the light from a chandelier overhead. They held hers for a long moment.

The waitress brought their desserts, and the moment broke. Rhiannon picked up her spoon, turning her attention to the dish before her.

After her first mouthful Gabriel asked, 'How is it?'

She forced herself to look at him, finding nothing but polite inquiry in his eyes. 'Very nice. Wonderful.'

He watched her take the next spoonful, then dug his own spoon into his gateau, asking, 'You don't have any trouble with the arm?'

'It was only a bruise.'

Deceptively casual, he said, 'Do you want to tell me why you were so frightened?'

Her hand tightened on the spoon. An unseen tremor passed through her. Without looking at him, after taking

a breath to school her voice to an even tone, she said,
'You startled me, that's all.'

Steadily she went on eating.

After a few mouthfuls, steering him away from her
life story, she asked, 'How did you start in the air-freight
business?'

He cast her a keen look but said, 'I fell into it more
or less by accident. I was working at the airport in the
customs department, and when a freight firm was threatened with receivership it seemed a good chance to buy
in and see if I could make a go of it.'

'You had the money for it?'

'The bank was good to me.' He grinned. 'Though I
had to convince them I could turn the business around
and make it a paying proposition.'

'You must have been very persuasive.'

He had his coffee cup in his hand, looking at her over
the rim. 'I can be very persuasive when I want to be.'

The disconcerting glint that sometimes lurked in his
eyes was there again. She had to make an effort not to
look away.

'And,' he said, 'my grandfather, bless him, offered to
guarantee me for a loan.'

So he'd had a fond grandparent, too. Maybe that had
helped when his parents split up.

Forking up a piece of gateau, Gabriel considered it.
'The old guy's gone now. He had a big globe on a brass
stand in his living room, and I remember him explaining
to me the concept of travelling around the world from
one place to another until you arrived back where you
started.'

'How old were you then?'

Gabriel swallowed the morsel of gateau. 'About five, I think. Ever since, a globe has reminded me of him. Maybe that's why the idea of buying the air-freight company appealed.'

He lifted his cup to his lips. Her gaze slipped to his throat, caught by the movement under his skin. She watched with fascination until he lowered the cup and she hastily turned her attention to her plate. 'It can't have been easy when you started,' she commented.

'It was a challenge.' He launched into a brief description of his career—the rocky beginning, the setbacks on the way, the eventual success—and she found herself caught up in his obvious enthusiasm.

Then he paused. 'I guess that's more than you ever wanted to know.'

'No. It's exciting.'

'Is that what excites you? Talking business?' His brows rose and his lips curved.

Rhiannon floundered. The innuendo was subtle and his eyes held laughter, but a flush rose from her throat and stung her cheeks.

Taking pity, he said, 'I'd call downhill skiing exciting, parachuting, hang-gliding…and a few other things.' For a moment a wicked gleam lit his eyes. 'But biz talk?' He shook his head. 'You haven't lived, baby.'

Rhiannon seized on the final word. 'I'm not a baby!'

'I'm nine years older than you,' he reminded her.

'Yes, Grandad.'

The gleam this time was retributive. 'And I'm not your grandad.'

Rhiannon gulped down a mouthful of hot coffee. He

didn't look like anyone's grandad. 'Have you done those things? I mean…downhill skiing, hang-gliding…?'

'And the rest?' A crease appeared in his cheek. He was trying not to laugh. Held by that shimmering gaze with its veiled, provocative challenge, Rhiannon was suddenly breathless.

But not frightened.

Gabriel didn't press her, to her great relief. This was too new a sensation to be taken at speed. He said nothing more until he'd demolished his gateau, then he sat back as she finished off her dish. 'What did you do with those tiles?'

She told him about the church commission, answering his questions regarding tools and techniques. When she mentioned using tiles from demolition sites, he said, 'The building next door to mine is being pulled down.'

'Oh?' She hadn't been near there recently.

'Maybe you should have a look.' Pushing away his empty cup, he asked, 'Do you want another?'

Rhiannon declined, not wanting any more coffee but curiously reluctant to move. She was, she realised dazedly, enjoying herself.

Only they couldn't stay here all night. She fumbled for her bag and put on her jacket. 'Thank you for this, it's been nice.'

Rain had fallen while they were in the restaurant, and when they stepped outside the pavement was wet and shining under the streetlights, the tyres of passing cars hissing on the road surface. Still warm from the day's sun, the asphalt steamed slightly.

'It could be slippery,' Gabriel said, his hand coming

to rest on Rhiannon's waist under the jacket. 'Is your car in the parking building?'

'Yes, but you don't need to come with me.'

'I'm going to pick up my car. And anyway, I wouldn't desert you in the street.'

She was very conscious of his barely perceptible touch on her waist all the way there. It wasn't an unpleasant sensation, and she didn't pull away until she took out her keys and unlocked her car.

Before she got in he stopped her with a light hold on her wrist, and her gaze flew to his face. A whole colony of butterflies seemed to have taken up residence in her stomach, and she conquered the urge to pull away, standing very still while consumed by conflicting emotions of dread and curiosity.

A faint frown appeared between Gabriel's brows. He bent his head quite slowly and brushed his lips against her cheek. 'Goodnight, Rhiannon.'

Then he opened the door for her, standing back when she started the engine.

Watching the tail-lights disappear down the ramp, Gabriel flexed his fingers, then folded them into his palm. He could still feel the warmth that had emanated through Rhiannon's thin blouse, and found himself fantasising about the smooth skin underneath the fabric, imagining tugging the garment from the imprisoning band of her skirt and running a finger along the groove of her spine, while he held her close…

It had taken considerable will-power to resist sliding his arm about her, resting his hand on her hip, nestling her shoulder under his. He'd felt the tiny tremor that seized her when he'd put his hand on her waist, and had made himself stop right there. In another woman he might have guessed the tremor indicated sexual awareness, but with Rhiannon…

He could hope, but she'd given no sign of welcoming his touch. And she'd been very composed, almost cool, since he'd walked into the gallery.

He went to the elevators, jabbing at the button.

Damn, she *had* been cool. Decidedly so. Cool and cagey. Not giving much away, except when he'd made an oblique, mildly sexual remark and she'd blushed like a schoolgirl.

So the coolness was a blind, a facade. Hiding what?

Fear. The word was stark, shocking.

He might never have suspected if he hadn't caught her off guard that first day, scaring her witless with a single, asexual touch and an offer of help. She hadn't been able to cover up so well then, her defences stripped for a few minutes by pain.

They were good defences.

The elevator doors slid open for him. A pretty young woman standing in the middle of the car gave him a small social smile as he entered and pressed the button for his floor. He could feel her covert glances but didn't return them.

Rhiannon in the same situation had backed into the corner.

She'd been anxious from the moment he entered.

The woman he was sharing with now stepped forward when the elevator glided to a stop at her floor, and gave him a lingering sidelong glance as she left. He had no urge to follow her before the doors closed again.

In the gallery, on her own turf, Rhiannon had been perfectly sure of herself with her customers, and her manner had scarcely changed when Gabriel approached, except for that slight, involuntary alteration in her expression, like an invisible glass mask.

The mask had slipped when she spoke of her work, but it went right back at any hint of masculine interest. As though she had no idea how to deal with it.

She didn't know how to flirt.

The doors opened and he stepped out. He smiled, unaware of the slightly tigerish quality of the smile.

Maybe he could teach her.

His purchase of the panel gave Gabriel an excuse to call at the gallery on Saturday, when Mosaica was open until two.

Ten minutes before closing time he found Rhiannon alone behind the counter, her head bent over a notepad.

'Hi,' he said, and she looked up, her eyes glazed for a moment.

When they cleared, her smile was uncertain. 'Hello.'

'You remembered?' He glanced over at the mosaic and the red sticker fixed to it.

Rhiannon seemed to gather herself, assuming a professional air. 'I was going to phone you on Monday and ask if you want it delivered.'

'I'll take it myself.'

'Now? Certainly.'

The door chime momentarily drew her attention to a middle-aged Japanese couple entering. Then she turned to the door standing ajar behind the counter and called, 'Peri?'

A broad-shouldered young man appeared, with smooth brown skin and large dark eyes, his black hair a mane of luxurious waves secured in a ponytail. A tie-dyed muscle shirt and purple leather pants hugged his lovingly honed chest and thighs, and he flashed a dazzling Tom Cruise smile at Rhiannon. 'Yeah, boss?'

'Mr Hudson's buying the mosaic over there. Could you pack it for him please?'

'Sure.' Peri ambled over to the piece and lifted it with effortless care before shouldering his way back through the doorway.

Her voice crisp, Rhiannon said to Gabriel's shirt-front, 'How did you want to pay?'

Reaching for his credit card, Gabriel experienced a flash of annoyance. From her manner, he could have been any stranger off the street. And seeing Peri had shaken him a bit. When Rhiannon mentioned an assistant he'd assumed a female one, not a hunky young guy who believed in making the most of his obvious assets.

It called into question all Gabriel's guesses and assumptions. If she didn't mind having *that* around every day she was hardly man-shy.

Just shy of certain men. Him, for instance.

Handing over the card, he studied her bent head as she processed the payment, remembering with a certain relief that she'd denied being in a relationship.

The Japanese couple were holding a murmured debate over a large wooden bowl, turning it over and running their fingers across the smooth finish. Rhiannon handed back Gabriel's card and said dismissively, 'Peri won't be long,' then went to speak to them.

Peri reappeared with the mosaic encased in sturdy

cardboard. 'Here you are, mate. I mean, sir!' He threw a comical glance at Rhiannon, but she was concentrating on the tourists, who didn't have much English. 'Want me to carry it? How far to your car?'

'No thanks,' Gabriel assured him shortly, not keen on following all that splendid musculature along the street. 'Just leave it here for now. I'm waiting to speak to your boss.'

'Sure.' Peri leaned the parcel against the end of the counter, giving him a rather sharp glance.

The couple decided to buy the bowl and, as they approached the counter with Rhiannon, she asked Peri to find a box and prepare it for posting.

While he bore the bowl off to the back room and Rhiannon patiently deciphered where the couple wanted it sent and took their payment, Gabriel stood by. After they had bowed their way out, she turned to him and indicated the wrapped mosaic. 'Is Peri going to carry that for you?'

She made to turn, presumably to call the assistant, and Gabriel reached out a hand but dropped it before his fingers touched her arm. 'I don't need Peri.' As she paused, he said, 'Have you eaten?'

'On Saturday we're usually very busy, and I don't bother until the shop closes.'

'Have something with me?'

'Why?'

Hadn't she ever heard of a date? He raised his brows and she looked flustered, biting her lip as her cheeks coloured.

Gabriel went to Plan B. 'I want to discuss a possible commission.'

Her eyelids flickered. 'What kind of commission?'

'Let me buy you a late lunch and we can talk about it.'

Her gaze lowered, and he saw the front of her blouse—teamed with dark green jeans—flutter as she took a breath. Then she raised her head and her eyes met his. 'All right.'

Gabriel was unprepared for the surge of triumph that made him want to grab her and kiss that gorgeous, tempting mouth. Instead he nodded and said, 'When you're ready.'

He found them an umbrella-shaded outdoor table at a café-bar. Rhiannon was glad to be offered the choice instead of going inside.

Over her Niçoise salad and Gabriel's curried kumara fritters he asked her, 'How long has Peri been with you?'

'Since I moved into the new place. I'd sold some carvings for him over the last couple of years, and he helped out before Christmas.'

'He's a carver?'

'His uncle taught him traditional Maori carving, and Peri's particularly interested in incorporating Maori motifs into modern design. But it doesn't pay enough to live on, and I figured I'd need an assistant when I moved into town, so I offered him the job.'

Peri had jumped at it, and she'd had no qualms about employing him.

Gabriel's look was oddly penetrating. 'I guess he's an asset to the shop.'

'He's keen, and strong.' Some of their stock, like the mosaic Gabriel had bought, was heavy and awkward;

she'd been glad of Peri's muscle. 'And he did his degree in art.'

Gabriel nodded, spearing a potato chip with his fork.

Rhiannon ate a shiny black olive and carefully placed the stone on the side of her plate. 'What's the commission you wanted to talk about?'

Reminding himself he'd told her it was a business lunch, Gabriel said, 'There's a blank concrete wall in the Angelair Building.' There was, since yesterday when he'd decided the huge tapestry hanging there was dusty and dated, and had it taken down. 'It needs some kind of artwork—like a mosaic.'

If he'd thought she'd jump at the opportunity to decorate the pride of his company, which had won a building industry award, he would have been wrong. She went very still, her fork poised with another olive on it. 'Why me?' she asked quietly.

Because I can't get you out of my mind. Because he wanted to pin her down, make sure she couldn't easily escape him while he delved under that fragile shell she adopted in public, and discovered what was beneath it. Because he wasn't sure that she wouldn't back away from him when she found out just how intensely he wanted to know her—in every sense of the word.

And because he had a hunch his supposedly irresistible charm wasn't going to work its magic with this woman.

He said, 'I like your work.'

'You want an unknown artist to do this?' She sounded sceptical.

'I've found out quite a lot about you, and—'

'*What?*' The fork in her hand lowered, and the skin on her cheeks went taut and pale. 'How?'

'Just by asking around,' he answered, pausing as her eyes widened and darkened, 'among people in the art scene.' And in the business world. Anywhere he could think of. Alerted by her reaction, he didn't mention how many feelers he'd put out in various directions. 'You're a young artist to watch, they said.' Which was about all he'd been able to discover.

She looked surprised, but the colour gradually returned to her face. Pushing her fork into her salad, she stirred the frilled lettuce leaves. 'Wouldn't you rather have someone who's a big name?'

'I'd get more satisfaction out of sponsoring an emerging artist.' He smiled at her. 'When you're famous I can say I spotted your talent early.'

'What if I never become famous?'

'Don't you believe you will?'

'I haven't really thought about it. I just like doing what I do.'

She'd told him she wasn't driven by ambition, despite her successful retail business. What did drive her? Love for her art? Or perhaps a simple need for money. He might turn that to useful account. 'Will you consider my proposal? I expect to pay a good price for it.'

'I don't have a lot of time right now, with the new gallery, and I have to finish my present commission.' She still seemed uneasy.

'I can wait.' If he had to. Not naturally patient, Gabriel had learned that sometimes patience was necessary in order to get what he really wanted. Deferred gratification, they called it. He had the distinct impression that Rhiannon had been deferring for a long time.

Absently stirring her salad again, she inquired, 'What size is the space?'

'Approximately three by five metres.'

Her eyes lifted. 'That big?'

He saw the spark of interest in her expression and pressed his advantage. 'Roughly. It's not flat, and it curves up at one end. I can show you after lunch if you have the time.'

Rhiannon picked out another olive with her fork and stared down at it as if it were a crystal ball. 'All right,' she said at last. 'I'll have a look.'

Gabriel let her into the foyer of the Angelair Building, pressing a button on a remote control to disable the alarm.

An elegant central stairway rising before them dominated the space, flanked by ground-floor businesses, their doors firmly closed. Gold lettering on a glass-enclosed board proclaimed that the Angelair offices were on the third floor while other firms occupied the remainder of the building.

'Up there.' Gabriel waved toward the stairs. Halfway up, the flight divided and curved around a convex, half-circular concrete wall, the top edge shaped upward from right to left.

'The central lift shaft is behind it,' Gabriel said. 'The other side is glass.'

She vaguely remembered it from visiting the building in the past. An architectural showpiece, although there were more conventional elevators at the rear of the shopping arcade.

'Could you do a mosaic there?' Gabriel asked.

'It would be a challenge.' Both in design and execution. 'And expensive,' Rhiannon warned, but with a stirring of excitement.

'Not a problem.'

Climbing the stairs, she asked, 'I suppose you'd like a design relating to your business, since your firm owns the building?' She went to the wall, raising her eyes to gauge the height, and stroked a hand along the curve, getting a feel for it. The finish wasn't too smooth to take a bonding agent, she noted.

'That would be good.' Gabriel spoke absently, watching the movement of her hand. Then he transferred his intent gaze to her face. 'But not a replica of the company logo.'

Rhiannon contained her smile. 'That's a relief.'

'You don't like our logo?'

'It isn't that I don't like it, but I don't want to reproduce someone else's design.'

'I was thinking of something more imaginative. Unique.'

'It will take some planning, and I can't work on it full time.'

'I told you I'm prepared to wait for what I want. And I think you can give me that.' His eyes were intent, and something in their expression made her breathing momentarily uneven. She had a peculiar sense that she was standing on the brink of some possibly hazardous edge, not on a solid marble landing.

Forcing her mind to practicalities, she banished the

bizarre fantasy. 'It will have to be done outside business hours.'

'All the better. Less disruption to traffic on the stairs.'

'I'd need a scaffold. I'm afraid that will take some room.'

'Hm.' He glanced up at the wall. 'Of course. We'll organise that. I'll talk to the guys who did the scaffolding next door when they started the demolition. They might like another small job.'

'Which firm is doing the demolition? I'd like to get hold of them and ask if I could have any damaged tiles.'

He wrote it down for her, and then said, indicating the wall, 'What do you think?'

There was no logical reason to turn down a promising commission. Gabriel was willing to pay out good money, the concept was exciting, and the exposure in a prominent position to hundreds of people entering the building every day would surely boost her reputation and perhaps bring more commissions. If she ever got to earn enough from her art, she could hire extra staff for the gallery and spend more of her time creating new works.

'If you're sure it's me you want,' she said, taking the plunge, 'then I'd like to take it on.'

He smiled as though she'd amused him. 'I'm sure I want you, Rhiannon.' His voice was low and there was a note in it that sent a spiral of peculiar, astonishingly pleasurable sensation down her spine.

Making her own voice crisp, she said, 'Do you have any definite ideas?'

His lips momentarily curled upward, his brows rising a fraction, but he said, 'About the design? That's up to you. But I'd appreciate some consultation.'

'Of course. I could make some sketches, and work out an estimated price and time frame before we go ahead.'

'I'll be looking forward to it.' He sent her a slow smile, almost intimate, and her breath hitched for an instant.

She put a hand on the smooth polished stair rail to steady herself, and began to descend, watching her feet.

Gabriel came to her side, his hands nonchalantly buried in his pockets. 'Maybe fate brought us together,' he said. 'The perfect match.'

Her step faltered, and swiftly he turned, an arm stretched across in front of her, his hand closing over the railing just below hers. He was one step down from her and their eyes were level. 'You and my blank wall,' he said. 'Are you all right?'

'Yes.' But her heart was jumping.

He'd thought she might fall, she realised. He wasn't trapping her.

He didn't move away instantly. 'You're safe,' he said, 'with me.'

Rhiannon swallowed. 'I wasn't falling.'

His smile was enigmatic and a little tight. 'I wouldn't mind, and I'm here to catch you.'

'I don't need to be caught.' Her throat felt as though there were a tiny moth helplessly imprisoned there.

'And don't want to be.' Gabriel spoke slowly, his eyes searching her face.

Rhiannon shook her head, not trusting her voice. New sensations bewildered her; a kind of excitement that was half fear and half something else, absolutely alien to her.

Dizzying warmth started at her toes and weakened her knees, rising to heat her cheeks and dry her mouth. She moistened her lips and Gabriel's gaze became riveted on them. Her heartbeat increased to suffocation point.

Then he said, his voice oddly muffled, 'So. We'd better get out of here.'

He went just ahead of her and she hurried down the remainder of the steps, ignoring the hand he offered when he reached the bottom.

He didn't comment on that, but something flared in his eyes, and Rhiannon didn't dare speak until he let them out of the building, using a side staff door down a short flight of concrete steps. 'This way it's a shorter walk back to your gallery,' he explained as he re-armed the alarm.

'You'll want to collect your mosaic,' she realised.

Once there she unlocked the door and stood by while he hoisted the bulky package into his arms.

'I'll let you know when I've had time to consider your project,' she told him.

'Aren't you leaving now?'

'I have stuff to do here.' She was still setting up the back room so she could do mosaics there.

'I'll see you again, then.' Gabriel smiled into her eyes, and then she was watching him stride away from her.

It was seconds before she roused herself to turn the other way and head for the back of the gallery.

Several times in the next few days Rhiannon almost phoned Gabriel's office to tell him she couldn't take on his project after all.

She was too discomfited around him, too aware of the frailty of the protective barriers she'd painstakingly built about herself.

He was the first man who had seriously threatened them.

She didn't know how to deal with the occasional gleam in his eyes, the crease of amusement in his cheek when he made some remark that seemed to hold a hidden meaning, only to give her a bland look when she became flustered, allowing her to pretend she hadn't noticed.

The evening he'd escorted her to her car after their coffee and cake, when he bent his head and she'd known he intended to kiss her, she'd stood like a possum caught in headlights, giving him no hint of reciprocation, no encouragement, and he'd deflected the kiss to her cheek.

Hours afterwards she'd fancied she could still feel the warmth of his lips on her skin.

It's called sexual attraction, she acknowledged with dawning surprise on Thursday morning, as she knelt on the floor of the workroom, packing a large glass vase into a shipping box. *A normal, healthy emotion.*

She sat back on her heels, incongruously struck by the revelation. It was several minutes before she roused herself.

After taping the box she reached for an air-freight label, peeled off the backing and smoothed the label with its familiar embossed angel wings onto the box. Her finger traced its outline.

Gabriel. The name of an angel, but angels were sexless, genderless. And Gabriel Hudson was all male.

Rhiannon had recognised that at their first meeting. Her predictable reaction had been alarm, but when he'd shown his concern after her fall the alarm was tempered by other less expected emotions, so foreign to her that she hadn't at first recognised them.

She was attracted to Gabriel. Not just distantly, aesthetically appreciative of his quite spectacular good looks, but physically affected.

And he'd quietly but unmistakably signalled that he found her…at least interesting.

An echo of the shock recoil she'd felt when he'd told her he'd 'asked around' about her sent out a warning signal. Reaching for a felt-tip pen, she waited a moment to steady her hand before writing an address on the Angelair label.

She'd been mistaken about his reason. Gabriel had wanted to know if she was good enough at her craft to work on his mural. That was natural, and perfectly legitimate. She couldn't go through life being suspicious of the motives of every male who crossed her path.

Fear was a prison. Maybe this was her chance to break out of it. Many women of her age had already had several lovers.

The pen slipped in her fingers, making a smudge. *Lovers?*

She tightened her grip, took a shaky breath and completed the label with care as the door chime indicated someone had entered the shop and she heard Peri offer his help.

Gabriel hadn't suggested he wanted to be her lover. Was she was reading too much into the warmth of his smile, the lurking appreciation in his eyes? Perhaps she'd mistaken simple courtesy and his unnecessary remorse for reciprocation of her own tentative and muddled feelings.

That would be a change. She stifled a nervous laugh. After all, Gabriel Hudson must have his pick of glamorous women, and although Rhiannon was aware she had been given an attractive face and figure, she made little effort to enhance them beyond meticulous grooming. 'You could wait until you're asked,' she muttered aloud, with a small grimace.

And if Gabriel did ask her to be his lover?

Her head jerked up. She had to still a flutter of panic. She could always say no.

Standing, she paused, slightly dizzy. Real women, women in charge of their own lives, as she was desperately determined to be, didn't turn their backs on opportunity.

She'd thrown herself into proving she could cope in business. Leasing the new gallery had shown she was capable of breaking out of her comfort zone. She had to learn to do that in her private life.

The gallery was busy until late afternoon, and when the pace slackened Rhiannon sent Peri home early, as she often did to make up for his not having a proper lunch-break. At the end of the day custom dwindled, everyone intent on hurrying home.

After five only one person came in, and left without buying anything. At ten minutes to six Rhiannon decided it wouldn't hurt to shut up shop a little early, and she was at the door when Gabriel appeared.

'Closing already?' he inquired, glancing at his watch.

Rhiannon paused, her hand on the latch. 'I never turn away a customer.'

'May I come in, then?'

She stepped back, leaving the door open. 'We have some new glassware by a South Island artist.' She waved to the display.

Gabriel hardly looked at the stand. 'Actually I wanted to talk to you.'

'About your commission?' she asked quickly, her startling discovery of this morning making her self-consciously afraid he might read her mind.

He said, after a second, 'Have you had time to give any thought to it?'

'Not a lot.' She'd been giving an inordinate amount of time to thoughts about him, though. 'I have some tentative ideas.'

'Don't let me rush you.'

'You're not rushing me.'

'I'm trying not to.' He gazed around the shop almost as though searching for inspiration. 'You've sold another of your mosaics?' he queried. The place where it had been was now filled by an exquisite appliqué hanging.

'We had a busy day.'

'Is that why you were closing early? You're tired?'

'Partly. And I want to visit my father before I go home.'

'I won't keep you, then.'

'I need to talk to you,' she admitted. 'I'd like to know what your thoughts are before I get too carried away. Just a moment.'

She went to the back room, and returned with a sheet of paper, placing it on the counter between them. 'I found this on the Internet. The Angel Gabriel, from an old Russian icon.'

He shot her a questioning look before turning his attention to the picture. 'You told me you weren't keen on replicas.'

'I'm not suggesting that, but I'd like to use the colours and some elements of the picture as a starting point.'

The archangel was depicted against a sky-blue background within a terracotta frame edged with crimson and blue. His long-sleeved garment was deep aqua green, the sleeves etched with gold light, and a softly crimson robe swathed his shoulder and lower body. In one hand he held a flower stem bearing a single red rose. She loved everything about it except that.

Gabriel looked up. 'The colours are great. Quite subtle but rich.'

'I'm glad you approve.'

He smiled at her, and a gleam lit his eyes. 'Oh, I approve, Rhiannon,' he drawled, 'very much.'

Rhiannon lowered her gaze, picking up the printout. 'Then I'll work on using this, but I'll need to measure the space before I go much further.'

'Sure. When would you like to do that?'

'Anytime, really, out of business hours. I'll have to get a stepladder from somewhere.'

'Leave it to me. Anything else?'

'No, I'll bring a tape measure.'

'Tomorrow—or is that too soon?'

'It isn't too soon. I can't work here on the triptych I'm doing, but I may have time to do some preliminary sketches for you when we're not too busy.'

'I'll expect you then, after six.'

Gabriel met her as arranged at the side door and they entered the lobby and climbed the main stairs together.

Someone had already placed a stepladder on the wide landing, and when they reached it he said, 'Can I help?'

She had changed into jeans before leaving the gallery, not fancying climbing a ladder in a skirt. But she said, 'If you can hold the tape at the top?'

When they were done Gabriel leaned against the stepladder while Rhiannon noted the final measurement. Then she looked up at the wall, thoughtfully trapping the end of the pen between her teeth.

'Problem?' he asked.

'Mm, calculating the degree of the curve. I may need to make a model so I can tell what's visible from different angles.'

'Would the original plans of the building help? I have them in my office.'

'You do?'

'I guess I should have thought of that before. All the measurements will be there.'

'I would have checked them myself anyway. Plans have been known to alter during construction.' She was still studying the wall, adding absently, 'But I'd like to see them.'

'Come on up then,' he said.

'Now?' She snapped to attention.

Gabriel's head tilted slightly. 'No time like the present,' he suggested gently, his eyes questioning her hesitation.

Rhiannon stilled. Being alone with him in his office was no different from being alone with him here in the spacious foyer, she told herself. His manner since she'd arrived had been perfectly neutral. She had no reason to refuse.

Nearby a loud crash and a rumble, accompanied by a slight tremor under their feet, made them both turn toward the sound. The demolition team next door were working late.

'This building is quake-proof,' Gabriel assured her as they climbed the stairs. 'A few falling bricks aren't going to do it any harm. Did you get any tiles from them?'

'I phoned the manager. He didn't want anyone going onto the site, but they did give me a few bits they'd fished out of the rubble.'

After passing through an outer reception area Gabriel motioned her into his office, a large room decorated in cream and brown with discreet touches of dark gold, and dominated by a desk on which a laptop computer sat among piles of paper.

She thought of her own office-cum-workroom-cum-storage space, which had seemed blessedly large and airy when she leased the High Street premises. Now her small desk shared the space with an even smaller table, two chairs and her wide work bench, plus a pyramid of display plinths not in current use, and various boxes piled to the ceiling.

'Something funny?' Gabriel inquired.

She hadn't realised her momentary amusement was showing. 'I was admiring your office.'

'I like it. It's functional and works well.'

And also sparely elegant. They crossed a thick mocha-coloured carpet toward a corner where a pair of comfortable sofas had been arranged at right angles to each other with a low, square table before them.

Instead of taking the seat he indicated, Rhiannon

looked about. 'You must have had a good interior designer.'

'I don't hire people whose work isn't good.'

'Should I be flattered?'

Gabriel smiled. 'There's no flattery in choosing the best person for the job.'

'I hope you won't be disappointed.'

'I'm sure you won't disappoint me, Rhiannon.' Slanting a glance at her, he offered, 'Coffee?' He switched on a machine nearby.

'Thanks.'

Several framed architect's sketches of the building hung on the walls, along with photographs of aeroplanes and groups of people. And, over the doorway facing the desk, the mosaic Gabriel had bought from her.

'Oh!' she said. 'I thought you'd taken that home.'

On his way to a built-in storage bank, Gabriel glanced back. 'I spend more of my waking hours here.' Taking a thick roll of plans from a cupboard, he briskly rolled them the other way to straighten them before laying them on the table. 'One of these may help.'

As she sat down he went to the coffee machine and came back with two steaming cups.

He handed her one and sat on the other sofa, regarding her from beneath lowered lids.

Rhiannon took a scalding sip of coffee and leaned forward to study the plans.

Gabriel did the same, sorting through the sheets until they found the relevant one.

He helped her check the plan against her measurements, and began rolling up the sheets of paper. 'Will it bother you if I watch you work sometimes? I'd like to follow your progress.'

It would bother her, but not seeing him for days on end hadn't stopped him intruding into her thoughts too often for comfort. Maybe familiarity would breed contempt—or something like that. 'No,' she lied. 'After all, you're paying for it.' So she could hardly refuse.

He'd soon get bored anyway, she guessed. It wouldn't be too different from watching paint dry.

He snapped a rubber band onto the roll of paper. 'Do you have any idea yet of costs?'

'I'll be able to give you a quote shortly, now that I have the exact size. But it won't come cheap,' she warned. 'To get the colours I'll probably need to buy new tiles, not rely on what I can find among used ones.'

'I'm not interested in cheap.' He put aside the rolled paper and leaned back. 'I've always paid whatever's necessary to get what I want.'

He looked relaxed, lounging with one arm along the back of the sofa, but a glint in his eyes made her gulp for breath and rush into speech.

'Suppose I overcharged you?'

The disquieting glint intensified, and his eyes narrowed further. 'I'm not stupid, Rhiannon. You won't cheat me.'

He'd made inquiries regarding her expertise. Had he also checked out her honesty?

Or perhaps it was a warning—no one got away with cheating him, she guessed.

Somehow it was important to know. Giving herself no time for second thoughts about discretion, she said baldly, 'You trust me?'

It was a moment before he answered, 'Yes.' Then he asked quietly, 'Do you trust *me?*'

Rhiannon blinked, and to hide her confusion drank some more coffee. 'I'm sure I can count on being paid for my work,' she said. 'Angelair has a reputation for integrity.'

She noted the slightest movement of his lips, but she wouldn't have called it a smile. His eyes cooled. 'That wasn't quite I meant,' he said, mildly enough, even as a certain rigidity in his expression caused her a flicker of apprehension. 'I'm talking about our personal relationship.'

The blunt approach cut through her evasion. Trying to summon a suitable reply, all she came out with was, 'Do we have one?'

'I certainly intend to. I thought that was understood.'

Rhiannon shot him a startled glance, and was shaken by the expression on his face—the steady gaze challenging her to duck the issue, his jaw inflexible, the curve of his mouth less a smile than a potent promise.

Taking fright, she stiffened, her chin lifting. 'Are you saying the commission depends on an *understanding* between us?'

It was a second before he reacted at all. Then she saw a tightening of his mouth, the skin around it seeming to pale. He stood up so abruptly she flinched inwardly, but instead of moving towards her he took several strides away, then turned at the desk, thrusting his hands into the pockets of his trousers. 'I'm not in the habit of blackmailing women.' Despite his rigid control she knew he was deeply, dangerously angry. 'I've already made my decision about the mosaic and I'll stick by it, unless you demand an outrageous price.' He cast her an almost threatening glance, as if daring her to use that as a ruse to get out of it. 'If you like we can draw up a contract right now.' He went to the other side of the desk and pulled out a drawer, tossing a sheaf of paper and a pen onto the polished surface.

Rhiannon put down her own cup and rose to her feet. 'That isn't necessary,' she said. 'I said I'd provide a quote first.'

For a moment he didn't move, staring down at the writing materials in front of him. Then he looked up, chillingly aloof, and in clipped tones said, 'As you wish.'

Across the room their eyes clashed. She took a step out from behind the coffee table and stopped, her fingers worrying each other until she deliberately untangled them. 'I'm sorry,' she said.

After a moment his mouth twisted briefly and his expression thawed. 'Apology accepted. And returned,' he added. 'I shouldn't have put you on the spot. I'm not usually so clumsy.'

'You're not clumsy.' If anything he was too sophisticated, too knowing. She was excruciatingly aware that his experience in the sexual minefield far outweighed hers.

One dark eyebrow rose just a fraction. 'Thank you. I'll try to live up to that in future.' His mouth curved. 'I like being with you. I'd like to be with you often, get to know you. But of course, if you don't feel the same way…'

She could turn him down. And he'd walk away…wouldn't he?

Astonishingly, it was the thought of him walking out

of her life that brought a clutch of dread to her throat. Some deep part of her knew she would be missing a chance that might never come again.

'If I'm anathema to you,' Gabriel prompted as the silence lengthened, 'now is the time to say so.'

Rhiannon dared a small smile, and even more daringly said, her voice coming out low and husky, 'You're not anathema to me.'

His expression lightened. 'No?' He walked around the desk, but stopped in front of it and leaned back, folding his arms. 'So what's the story, Rhiannon?'

Her gaze shifting to one of the plans on the wall, she said, 'I'm not very good at...relationships.'

'You've been in a bad one? More than one?'

She made herself look at him, only fleetingly. 'I just...don't have much interest in men.'

Gabriel looked sceptical. 'You're a beautiful woman. There must have been men in your life...or at least men who were interested in being a part of it.'

Rhiannon lifted a shoulder. 'I've been building up my business, there hasn't been time for much else.'

The frown reappeared. 'So, the sixty-four-thousand-dollar question,' he said softly. 'Are you interested in me?'

It was a moment of truth. Rhiannon felt herself go pale, her cheeks and temples cooling. Dizzy with foreboding and the now-familiar rush of adrenaline that she associated with Gabriel Hudson, she admitted, 'I...like you.'

'Like?' His brows rose, and then he laughed.

She must sound incredibly naive. He had no idea how

difficult this was for her. Lifting her chin, she met his eyes with a hint of defiance.

The laughter died and he stared back at her intently, his gaze not shifting from her face. Then he held out a hand to her. 'Come here,' he invited.

Rhiannon swallowed, and her lips parted even as her eyes widened.

He was asking her to make the first move. And after a second of stunned indecision she did, taking one hesitant step, then another, as if she were walking on the edge of a precipice, where a single slip might be fatal.

Two steps away she brought up her hand and it found his outstretched one, his strong fingers closing about hers. And instead of panic she felt only a sensation of safety and warmth, almost shocking in its intensity.

Half expecting to be hauled into his arms, she was surprised again. He slowly lifted her hand and bent his head to press a kiss against the back of it, then turned her wrist to his mouth and the tip of his tongue found the tiny, hurrying pulse.

A shaft of pure heat arrowed through her body, and she gave a gasp.

Gabriel raised his head, the glitter in his eyes making her pulses race even faster. Taking her other hand, too, he drew her inexorably closer, until their bodies lightly touched, his thighs against hers, her breasts brushing his shirt. Even through their clothes she could feel the heat emanating from him. She tried to breathe lightly, evenly, and didn't dare look at him, fixing her gaze on the Venetian blinds behind him that filtered the light from outside.

'Rhiannon?' His breath stirred tendrils of hair at her forehead.

Her eyes felt heavy-lidded but she made herself look at him—so close she could discern the light beard-shadow on his determined chin before she raised her eyes to his, and saw herself reflected in the dark centres.

'Rhiannon,' he said again, 'would you like me to kiss you?'

Alarm flared and died. She was suddenly very calm and sure. His mouth was close to hers, its contours beautiful in a wholly masculine way, firm but not narrow, decisive yet promising tenderness.

Scarcely above a whisper, against the thunder that was the sound of her racing heart, she said, 'Yes.'

CHAPTER THREE

IT WASN'T at all as Rhiannon expected. For what seemed the longest time Gabriel didn't move, just looked down at her as if making sure she meant what she said.

He didn't wrap her in an embrace, but laced his fingers through hers at her sides and bent his head again to touch her lips lightly, briefly, with his own, then drew back a fraction. She had time for a pang of surprised disappointment before he did it again, but this time he let his lips rest on hers for a moment, and when he lifted his mouth he returned it almost instantly to hers, a little more firmly, exerting just enough pressure to part her lips.

She had never thought a man's mouth could be so soft, so tenderly nurturing, as if he wanted to give rather than take. As if her mouth was something delicate and precious that required a great deal of care and attention. As if *she* was...

She had never been kissed that way before.

When he raised his head again and looked down at her with a faintly quizzical expression, she could only stare back at him dazedly, until he loosed one of her hands and gently ran a thumb over her mouth. 'You could kiss me back,' he suggested, with a hint of amusement.

Ashamed to admit she didn't know how, Rhiannon flushed. To hide it, she ducked her head and turned from him, pulling her fingers from his and pretending her hair needed to be smoothed into place. 'I have to go,' she mumbled.

When he moved she shied away, but he was only going to the sofa to collect the bag she'd left there. He handed it to her, his gaze enigmatic. 'I take it you have things to do tonight.'

'I promised to go grocery shopping with my flatmate.'

'You have a flatmate? Another artist?'

'Janette's a nurse.'

'Ah,' he said. 'Janette.'

He saw her out of the building and into her car that she'd parked just across the street, taking advantage of a space left by a rush-hour commuter. Before closing the door he said, 'I'm due to fly to Australia tomorrow to visit our Sydney office, but when I get back I'll be in touch.'

A breathing space, she thought, relief swamping a pang of disappointment as she turned the key in the ignition.

She could scarcely believe what had happened minutes ago.

All the way home she kept remembering the kiss, reliving it with astonished pleasure and a measure of delicious disquiet, until an impatient motorist behind her reminded her a red light had changed to green, and she wrenched her mind back to her driving.

Gabriel phoned her at the end of the following week, during a slack period at the gallery. 'I just got back last night,' he said, 'and my secretary's handed me a couple of complimentary tickets for the opening of the African dance spectacular tonight. If you're free would you care to join me and see the show?'

'Tonight?'

'I realise it's short notice. If you're busy—'

'No.' Making a decision, her voice sounding as if it were someone else's, she said, 'I mean, that…would be nice. Thank you.'

'Can I call for you at home?'

'No, meet me here,' she said quickly. 'What time?'

'How about seven fifteen? Then we'd have time for a snack before the show, and perhaps we can have supper afterwards.'

As she put down the receiver Peri asked curiously, 'A date?'

'The African dancers.'

'Supposed to be a good show. Tickets are hard to get, I heard.'

'Gabriel has complimentary ones.'

'Gabriel Hudson?' Peri's brows rose. 'What are you going to wear?'

She glanced down at her straight tan skirt and light green blouse. 'I won't have time to go home.'

Peri looked disapproving. 'Sweetie, for Gabriel Hudson you need something special. Why don't you duck out at lunchtime and find yourself a glam outfit? Tell you what, why don't we both duck out? Left to yourself you'll get something boring that doesn't do you justice.'

Rhiannon knew her clothes were boring. She didn't enjoy calling attention to herself. 'No,' she said. 'I can't do that.'

'Come on, Rhee, there are a dozen boutiques within

two minutes of here where we can find you some decent glad-rags. How many customers might we lose in half an hour? One? Two, maybe?'

In the end she yielded, not admitting that the thought of shopping on her own for 'glad-rags' was a daunting one.

Peri had a wonderful time, rejecting anything that lacked colour or style, and finally giving the thumbs up to a simple, short-skirted aqua silk dress that he said was 'gorgeous with your eyes' and a peacock-blue satin jacket. The finishing touch was a pair of dark blue, side-buttoned high-heeled boots with a Victorian flavour.

'You look great,' he told her later when she had closed the gallery for the day, showered in the tiny bathroom attached to the office-cum-storeroom, dressed, and applied a little makeup, also bought under Peri's critical eye. He'd even stayed after locking up, ostensibly to view his handiwork but, she suspected, also to make sure she didn't chicken out and resume her everyday clothes.

'I feel like Cinderella,' Rhiannon confessed. 'This isn't me.'

'Of course it's you,' Peri said. 'The true you, the very attractive feminine you. You've been hiding your light under a pumpkin for too long.'

'A *pumpkin?*' Rhiannon laughed. 'That's a bushel, you idiot!'

He grinned back at her, reaching out a hand to arrange a strand or two of hair over her forehead and cheek. Then a rap on the glass door signalled Gabriel's arrival. Peri dropped his hand, standing back to examine her with a satisfied air. 'Shall I let him in?'

'Thank you.' Busy picking up the beaded satin clutch

purse that Peri had insisted she needed, she missed the sharp glance and curt nod that Gabriel gave the other man as he entered, and when she turned was mystified at Peri's gleeful expression before he murmured, 'I'll leave you to it, Rhee,' and blew her a kiss, sauntering out the door.

But she couldn't miss the comprehensive glance Gabriel swept over her, or the appreciative gleam that lit his eyes. 'Ready for me?' he asked.

She nodded, wondering if she would ever be ready for this man. Tonight he wore a dinner jacket and dark pants with a dazzling white shirt, and he looked more handsome than ever.

'Do many people call you Rhee?' he asked.

'A few close friends. Does anyone call you Gabe?'

'Only my family. Feel free.'

'I'm not family.'

He regarded her pensively for a moment. 'Shall I get a taxi?' he asked.

'No, we can easily walk to the theatre.'

'In those shoes?' He smiled, glancing at her feet in their buttoned boots.

He had a point there. She didn't often wear such slender high heels, and it was quick of him to have noticed. Maybe he was experienced in the shortcomings of female fashion. The thought brought a renewed reminder of her own lack of experience with his sex.

'I'll be all right,' she assured him, going to the door and snicking the lock.

'Not that I don't like them,' he murmured, as he closed the door behind them.

'I dressed up for…for this.' *For you,* she'd been about to say.

Perhaps he guessed. 'It was worth the effort,' he said. 'You look stunning.'

'You look good, too.'

'Thank you very much,' he said gravely. 'I made an effort myself.'

When they reached the theatre and walked into the foyer Rhiannon was glad she had taken Peri's advice. Some people wore quite casual clothes, but it was the kind of casual that cost, and others glittered in sequins and silk, even jewels.

She and Gabriel attracted a few stares, she supposed because he was known to a lot of people, or perhaps just because he was so spectacularly good-looking. With his tall bulk beside her and his hand lightly encircling her arm she felt confident and safe as he guided her through the throng and, securing a small table for them, ordered wine and nibbles.

By the time they entered the auditorium and took their seats, she was beginning to enjoy herself.

At the end of the dynamic, non-stop performance of music and dance, her mind was filled with exotic images of colourful though often minimal costumes, beautiful human beings, and uninhibited, joyful and dramatic movement and sound. She emerged into the foyer feeling as if she had spent the last couple of hours in another world.

Someone hailed Gabriel and he introduced her to a man and woman, but she scarcely caught their names and had to make an effort to smile and listen to a few minutes' small talk before Gabriel steered her to a nearby restaurant.

The hostess pulled out a chair and Rhiannon sank into it as the woman promised a waiter would be with them in a minute.

Rhiannon adjusted her chair and found a space on the table for her bag. When she looked up Gabriel's gaze was on her, almost meditative. 'Some of those dances were rather raunchy,' he said. 'And the costumes…or lack of…you didn't mind?'

Rhiannon shook her head. 'Of course not. It was a wonderful show.'

'I guess artists don't have much room for prudishness.'

The wine waiter came and Gabriel asked Rhiannon what she'd like.

'I'll just have a glass of house red,' she said. 'I'll be driving home later.'

When the man had gone, Gabriel said, 'I was hoping you'd let me take you home.'

'My car's in the parking building. I don't want to leave it overnight.'

A faint scepticism flitted across his face but he seemed content to let her off the hook, talking of the show until their meals came, then switching to a discussion of other forms of art.

When they left the restaurant the street was quieter, although there were still people around and a steady stream of cars passed by.

As they walked over an uneven stretch of pavement her heel caught momentarily in a crack between flagstones and she stumbled, only saved by Gabriel's quick reflexes as he shot out a hand and gripped her arm, steadying her.

For a half second she was held within inches of his body, breathing in the scent of him. Her palm was against his chest, the warmth of his skin coming through the fabric of his shirt before she snatched her hand away.

Gabriel loosened his grip but retained a light hold on her arm. 'You okay?'

'Yes.' Except that her heart frantically jumping about. 'Thank you.'

'They might be sexy as hell, but those shoes are a hazard.'

'Sexy?' Involuntarily she looked down at the ankle-high boots.

'Sure. All those little buttons down the side... intriguing.' He cocked his head to one side. His eyes, lit by a nearby street lamp, teased. Then he sobered, searching her face, and his mouth turned down in a wry, silent apology.

Instinct urged her to duck the challenge, ignore the brief provocation and sidestep the incident.

But another, less familiar imperative rebelled against a cowardly retreat. She took a silent, hidden breath and forced her eyes to meet Gabriel's, saying lightly, 'You're not a foot fetishist, are you?'

It was worth it to see the flare of surprise in his eyes. Then he laughed delightedly, making her feel warm all over. 'Not a fetishist of any kind,' he assured her, surveying her with veiled curiosity. 'I just happen to like...your shoes.'

The pause, she knew, was no mistake. The crooked smile and the expression on his face told her so quite explicitly, stirring a whole pot full of mixed emotions—doubt, trepidation, but mostly a bubble of cautious euphoria. She could do this. Just like any other woman who'd been taken out, wined and dined by an attractive man, she could make light conversation, respond to compliments, exchange banter laced with subtle innuendo. All she needed was a bit more practice.

Gabriel seemed willing to help her with that.

When they resumed walking, his hand remained curled about her arm.

Her car was only two floors up, and when she declined to wait for the lift he accompanied her without comment.

Other motorists were slamming doors, starting motors, and heading for the exit. Gabriel opened Rhiannon's door as a carload of young men stopped behind them, yelling obscenities at someone too slow to get moving. Rhiannon flinched, and Gabriel urged her into the driver's seat, standing protectively by until the other car passed, belching exhaust fumes.

Then he bent, and turned her face up with a hand under her chin, pressed a quick kiss on her mouth and straightened, shutting the door.

The following morning he phoned her at the gallery. 'Are you busy tonight?'

'I've promised to help with a concert at Dad's nursing home.' The residents who were able to take part had been preparing for weeks, and even though her father's reactions were hard to gauge, he seemed to enjoy listening to music.

'Could we have lunch, instead, when you've finished at the gallery today?'

Tempted, she hesitated. 'I really have to work on my church commission this weekend if I'm to finish it by the due date.'

'Another time then,' he said after a moment.

'I guess so.' She probably sounded distracted; the gallery was buzzing with the largest Saturday morning crowd they'd had so far, and she was needed at the counter.

'I'll hold you to that,' Gabriel said. 'You'll let me know when you have some news about my mural?'

'Of course.'

She phoned him on Tuesday, saying, 'I have some sketches for you to see, when it suits you.'

'How about tonight?' he said promptly. 'We can discuss them over that dinner I promised you.'

Rhiannon hardly hesitated. 'All right. I'll be finished here before seven.'

'Do you have a preference for a particular style of food? Seafood? Maybe something exotic like Thai or Lebanese?'

'I'll leave that to you. I like them all.'

'A woman who's easy to please,' Gabriel said, as if it was novelty.

'That's not so rare, surely,' Rhiannon protested. 'I shouldn't think you'd have any trouble.'

It was the literal truth, a thought voiced without reflection, but Gabriel was silent for a moment, and then he laughed. 'Thank you. I do my best.'

Maybe she should have suggested a later time, Rhiannon thought, putting down the phone. She'd have to go in the clothes she was wearing unless she indulged in another hasty shopping spree. Today she'd put on a button-through, belted jade green dress with a stitched collar, and her shoes were medium-heeled moss green. A neat, smart outfit for business, and surely not unsuitable for dining out.

Most of her eating out was with women friends, and price was often a major consideration. She had no idea what kind of place Gabriel had in mind for tonight.

He arrived in a taxi, and ushered her into it. 'I hope you'll share a bottle of wine with me,' he said, 'and I don't want to risk driving afterwards.'

'I'm not dressed for anywhere fancy,' she warned.

'You look fine,' he assured her, his gaze making a leisurely survey. 'Quite beautiful.'

Even though he had wedged his broad shoulders into the corner of the seat, leaving plenty of space between them, Rhiannon noticed a whiff of the scent she had come to associate with him. It woke a strange feeling in her, warm and soft and liquid.

He asked after her father and Rhiannon said, 'He seems…contented.' Mostly he sat in a comfortable chair with a tiny smile on his face, his eyes innocent and empty. 'The staff are very good.'

'I guess that's some compensation for you.'

'Yes.' She wished she could have confided in her father, told him about Gabriel and the ambivalent, unfamiliar feelings he evoked, asked for advice. But although she talked to him about her daily life, hoping some of it entered his poor, damaged mind, his rare responses were irrelevant or inappropriate, and if she seemed troubled he would become agitated, distressing them both. She said, 'I've brought some sketches for you to look at. I'll show you when we get there.'

The restaurant he had chosen overlooked the harbour. They were seated by a window where people passed by, and beyond the roadway distant lights lit the dark waters of the Hauraki Gulf with shimmering golds, reds and greens.

While they waited for their meals, Rhiannon allowed him to top up her glass with the velvety red wine he'd ordered, and pulled out a couple of sketches. 'They're just ideas,' she said. 'I'm not ready to commit to anything yet.'

Gabriel flicked her a glance, and his cheek momentarily creased. 'I realise that.' Glancing at the pages she'd handed over, he said, 'I never asked how you came to take up mosaic in the first place.'

'I dropped a rather beautiful platter soon after I took over my grandmother's shop, smashed it beyond repair.' She paused, remembering. She'd been shaking and verging on tears at the inadvertent destruction, and a woman in the shop had stepped in with practical help. 'A customer suggested using the pieces in a mosaic. She volunteered to show me how, and once I began I was hooked on it.'

'Making a work of art out of something beautiful but…damaged?'

His gaze was almost uncomfortably percipient, as if he could see more than she was willing to expose. 'I don't always use broken pieces,' she said hurriedly. 'I can work with cut tiles, like the classical mosaic artists.' She'd taken some classes at an art school and learned varied techniques, tried them all.

'Which do you prefer?'

'Abstract patterns often work best with random shapes, but pre-cut tiles are good for precision and formality.'

Gabriel quirked an eyebrow at the evasion, but said only, 'I guess precision and formality are sometimes what you need.'

They weren't words that would appeal to him, she guessed. 'Your mosaic will be adventurous and bold,' she assured him. 'To reflect your outlook.'

He cocked his head, regarding her with narrowed eyes. 'Am I that easily read?'

Ducking the question again, Rhiannon said, 'Your advertising people have developed an image for Angelair and fixed it in the public mind.'

'And that's the image you have in your mind, of me?'

'You *are* Angelair, aren't you?'

'I'm a man, Rhiannon. Not just a company.'

She hastened to placate him. 'You can't help stamping your personality on the company you own.'

'As you've stamped yours on Mosaica?' he countered.

'I suppose, yes,' she agreed somewhat reluctantly, and reached for her wineglass.

Gabriel said blandly, 'I must have another look at the decoration around the Mosaica doorway.'

He was much too clever for comfort. Rhiannon lifted her glass so hurriedly that wine spilled over her hand and onto the table.

'Oh!' Hastily she put down the glass.

Gabriel snatched up a napkin and took her wrist in strong fingers, wiping her hand dry. Then he signalled a passing waiter and said to him quietly, 'We need a little cleanup here.'

When the man had fixed the spill and gone, Rhiannon was sitting with the napkin clenched in her lap. 'Thank you for the rescue,' she said.

'Did you get any wine on your clothes?'

'No.' Carefully she put the napkin the table. 'I'm sorry.'

'Why? No harm done.'

'I feel stupid.'

'You're not stupid, Rhiannon. Far from it.'

Rhiannon carefully picked up her glass again and drank the little wine that remained. When she'd put it down and licked the taste from her upper lip, she found Gabriel watching.

As his gaze tangled with hers she had a curious feeling that time hung in the balance, and their surroundings faded away. Then he slowly picked up the bottle and poured more wine for her.

Shaking off the bizarre impression, she said, 'What do you think of the drawings? They're only roughs but if you like the basic ideas I'll keep refining them.'

He turned his attention to them, and Rhiannon told herself to relax.

The wine helped, and the fact that the food when it came was delicious—fresh, and superbly cooked and presented.

Gabriel said, 'I like your ideas a lot, but how do you get from the Russian icon to a design like this? What's the creative process?'

She tried to explain as best she could, and when she

looked down at her wineglass, was surprised to find it was almost empty again.

Gabriel refilled it and asked, 'Shall we order another bottle?'

'I don't think so. Obviously it makes me babble.'

'You weren't babbling.' But he put the drawings aside and was soon fascinating her with a hair-raising account of recently getting a package to a Red Cross team in a war zone. Even Gabriel, as managing director, had been directly involved in pulling strings across several borders to ensure the safety of both package and courier.

Rhiannon said, 'Surely that's beyond your contract?'

'We pride ourselves on going the extra mile. There's no point in breaking our necks, maybe even risking a plane and pilot, to drop off a parcel at a deserted, shot-up airfield in the middle of a wasteland, and then washing our hands of it.'

'Don't you ever give up?'

He looked at her rather pensively, his eyes bluer than usual. 'When I put my mind to something giving up is hardly an option. If I can't get what I want one way, I'll keep trying others until I find the one that works.'

Rhiannon looked down at her wine, her fingers curling about the stem of her glass. A series of goose bumps rose on her skin.

'What's the matter?' Gabriel inquired softly.

'Nothing.' Deliberately she shook away the intrusive feeling. Paranoia would get her nowhere. Gabriel's determination went with who he was and what he'd done with his life. If he wasn't born with it, he'd had to develop it somewhere along the way. She shifted her gaze to him. 'You're very successful.'

His eyes searched her face, but he said only, 'So are you. I respect that.'

The comment warmed her. True, she had no desire to own a multi-million-dollar company as he did, but she'd come a long way since taking over a poky suburban handicraft shop as a nervous, inexperienced teenager.

She'd learned to deal with pushy salesmen, volatile artists and the odd aggressive customer or supplier, instead of falling apart and allowing them to walk all over her. Although she might feel sick afterwards, she could hold her own now and it became easier every time.

And she had avoided having to deal with men on a personal, intimate level.

Gabriel left her in no doubt that he was heading in that direction. Unknown territory for her, and more than a little scary.

She'd fought a long, lonely emotional battle, and won—put the nightmare behind her and made herself a solid, ordered life. But each new conquest revealed yet another problem, new demons to overcome.

Maybe Gabriel was the one to help her fight them. The archangel who would send the last of them to the underworld and finally set her free.

Involuntary she smiled, wondering how he'd feel about being so described.

A questioning eyebrow lifted in return. 'What are you thinking?'

Rhiannon shook her head. 'Nothing.'

Nothing she could tell him. Nothing she could tell anybody. The fleeting urge to engage Gabriel in her personal battle was a momentary weakness. This was her own private war, only to be won by her own strength and courage. No one could do it for her. She'd been down that road once and it was a dead end.

They lingered over coffee, but Rhiannon declined a second cup, and Gabriel looked at his watch. 'Do you fancy a short walk?'

The night air would be cool and refreshing, and she could do with the exercise after that meal. Walking at night was something she'd used to enjoy but didn't dare to do on her own.

As they crossed the road during a break in traffic, Gabriel caught her hand, and retained it when they gained the path on the other side.

Rhiannon didn't protest. She remembered the first time he'd touched her, covering her hand with his after she'd hurt herself on the stairs.

As they had been then, his fingers were warm and strong but his clasp was not so tight that she couldn't have tugged free. She found herself concentrating on the novelty of it, trying to analyse the experience and failing. She was feeling strangely floaty, and wondered if that was caused by the amount of wine she'd had. Usually she limited herself to less than two glasses. Somehow tonight she'd let herself be persuaded into three, not even including the one she'd spilt. Which probably meant Gabriel had drunk less than she had. A tiny suspicion nagged, but she deliberately ignored it, remembering her recent resolutions.

They strolled along the waterfront, a salty breeze cooling Rhiannon's face and smoothing her hair back. The water lapped at the stones below them, the streetlights turning the small waves to shot satin. A pohutukawa tree brushed Gabriel's hair as they passed under the bowed branches, the fallen red, spiky flowers making a carpet for their feet.

A night-time jogger passed them, breathing hard, a reflector belt gleaming about his waist, and he was followed by a briskly walking couple with a dog. On the road cars whizzed by.

A wisp of hair blew into Rhiannon's eyes, and she shook it away.

'You're not too cold?' Gabriel asked.

'No.' In fact she was deliciously warm, despite the seaborne breeze.

After a while they stopped, leaning on a seawall side by side to gaze at the moving water, the reflected lights, the faint glimmer of a few stars competing with the brighter glow of the city. Gabriel released her hand and she felt almost bereft.

'This is lovely,' she said.

Gabriel turned his head to look at her. 'Would it be too corny to say, so are you?'

Her heart thudded briefly. She moved, straightening and turning from him. The steady breeze gusted briefly, again blowing hair across her eyes, and she lifted a hand to brush it aside, shivering.

Gabriel moved closer, took her hand from her face and kissed her almost forcefully, quickly drawing back, but his hand still encircled her wrist. She remained still, a little startled but unafraid, and after a moment or two his other hand went to her waist, bringing her closer.

He kissed her jawline just under her ear, and slid his lips to her throat, then found her mouth again, this time with care and tenderness, his lips gently parting hers, sending a lick of exquisite flame darting through her.

She felt her mouth soften under his erotic ministrations. His hand pressed hers to his warm, hard chest and, following blind instinct, she moved closer to him, letting his arm slip further about her waist.

Then quick footsteps sounded on the pavement, and Rhiannon pulled away as the couple with the dog walked by arm in arm.

Gabriel gave a soft laugh, releasing her. 'I'll take you home,' he said, his voice thick, muffled. 'Unless you'd like to come to my place?'

Dumbly Rhiannon shook her head. One day maybe she would say yes, but she was nowhere near ready for that yet. And the kiss, brief though it had been, had set her heart thudding with mixed, disturbing emotions.

'I didn't think so.' But he didn't sound disgruntled. He turned to the roadway, raised an arm, and a passing cab swerved into the kerb.

'How do you do that?' Rhiannon wondered, her voice slightly shaky although she'd tried to sound casually flippant.

Gabriel laughed, the sound easing her disquiet. 'Sheer dumb luck. And maybe because I'm with a beautiful woman. Any cabbie would find you worth stopping for.'

'It doesn't work when I'm on my own,' she told him as they climbed in.

'Where to?' the driver asked.

She should have realised this was coming; her brain must be fuddled by alcohol—and Gabriel's company. If her car was parked in the city she'd have asked to be taken there but, having no bulky materials to carry, she'd left it at home, and caught a bus to save fuel and parking costs.

By the time she opened her mouth, Gabriel had filled the pause, giving her home address, then he settled back and took her hand in his between them.

Rhiannon felt her lifeless fingers enclosed again in his strong clasp as the cab made a quick U-turn. Shuddering with shock, she was too paralysed to pull away. It was moments before she could trust herself to speak, rather than scream the question that was racing crazily round and round in her head.

She didn't dare even look at him, and her voice came out thin and high, against a loud pounding in her temples. *'How do you know where I live?'*

CHAPTER FOUR

GABRIEL'S fingers tightened on her hand even as she tried to draw it away. He glanced at the back of the taxi driver's head, and after the tiniest pause said, 'Didn't you tell me?'

'No!' Rhiannon tugged angrily at his hold and at last he let go. She fought an urge to retreat into a corner of the seat and curl herself up in a defensive ball, or tell the taxi driver to let her out right now.

If she did that, Gabriel would follow her. At least here there was a third person, a potential ally. Maybe.

She straightened her back, willing herself to stay calm, be rational. It was difficult when her heart was hammering in an erratic rhythm and her mouth was desert-dry. 'I never tell clients my address.'

Gabriel didn't move. He'd folded his arms and was leaning into his own corner, half turned to face her. In the dark it was impossible to see his expression, the streetlights only intermittently lighting it in quick glimpses, making him a stranger. His voice low and very even, he said, 'I'd hoped I was something more than a client.'

Rhiannon took a gulping breath. 'How did you find it?'

'It's in the Angelair computer system. You told me you'd used our services.'

Of course. She couldn't lug heavy equipment and materials between the shop and her studio at home, so she'd often received and sent parcels with that address. Especially before she'd bought the station wagon.

Icy cold all over, she queried sharply, 'You looked it up?' Maybe he'd done it before. 'Is that how you usually get to meet women?'

'No!' He sat up. 'I was searching for something else and saw your name.'

'And memorised my address! You had no right!' she said fiercely.

After a moment he said, 'I did it without thinking. I'm sorry, Rhiannon. I don't want to upset you.'

'I'm not upset,' she lied. 'I'm furious! How dare you do that to me? It was unethical!'

She was right, Gabriel knew. Clients' addresses were privileged information, and he'd skin alive any of his staff caught using one for private purposes. When her name had come up on the list he was scanning, he'd automatically paused and skimmed the address, unable to stop himself, and from that moment it was indelibly fixed in his brain.

A rare shame invaded his psyche. He'd always considered himself honourable and honest—it was something he prided himself on in both his business and private life.

Of course he'd never intended to use the knowledge. Rhiannon had seemed to be waiting for him to tell the driver where they were headed, and he'd recited her address without giving it a second thought, forgetting how he had learned it.

'It wasn't deliberate,' he said. 'All I can do is apologise. Grovel, if you like.'

'I don't want you to grovel,' she said tightly. 'I just want to keep my privacy.'

'I promise you, I won't breach it again.' Instinctively he reached out his hand to her, then dropped it on the seat between them, inwardly cursing his inept handling of the situation. 'It was accidental, I swear.'

Rhiannon's stomach was churning sickly. Old memories chilled her through, so that instinctively she wrapped her arms about herself, hunched into her corner of the cab seat. She needed to think. Preferably away from Gabriel's disturbing presence. She turned her head, staring blindly out the window at the passing streetlights, the darkened houses, the occasional porch light blazing a welcome to late homecomers.

As if respecting her need, or perhaps mindful of the driver's silent presence, Gabriel too remained quiet and unmoving.

When the taxi halted outside her house he told the driver, 'Keep the meter running,' and followed Rhiannon along the short path to the door. The street was well lit—she'd made sure of that before moving in—and the small lawn bare of shrubs. A security light came on as they ascended the three steps to the porch.

Without looking at Gabriel, she put her key in the lock.

'I guess,' he said, 'you're not going to invite me in.'

She opened the door a fraction before reluctantly facing him. 'It was a nice evening, thank you.'

'It was a terrific evening,' he said regretfully, 'until I put my foot in it. Wasn't it?'

Her gaze slid away towards the waiting taxi. The driver wasn't visible. Gabriel didn't make a move to leave.

One lean male finger touched her cheek, then slipped under her chin, exerting the slightest pressure to make her look at him again. His eyes were dark and watchful. 'Don't let my stupidity spoil it.'

His thumb moved over lips, a light caress that sent an alarming tingle of sensation through her entire body, so that she deliberately stiffened it. Then he leaned forward and dropped a fleeting kiss on her brow. 'Goodnight, Rhiannon,' he said, and in the next second he was striding back down the path.

The following day Rhiannon was rearranging glassware on a shelf in the gallery when a voice behind her said, 'Ms Rhiannon Lewis?'

A delicate freeform vase in her hand, she turned to see a man in a leather jacket holding a sheaf of apricot-coloured roses. The vase slipped from her hand and smashed to pieces on the tiled floor.

The man stepped back with an exclamation, and Peri shot out from the back room.

'Hell!' the dismayed messenger said. 'I'm sorry! I didn't mean to give you a fright.'

'It's all right,' Rhiannon assured him, when she could speak and her heart had settled back into its normal position. 'Not your fault.'

'These are for you,' the man said, thrusting the bouquet towards her.

She stared at it, the scent rising from the beautiful blooms nauseating her.

Peri had reached her side, and looked up from surveying the damage. 'Here,' he said. 'I'll take them.'

The carrier relinquished them with relief. 'Sorry about that,' he said again, backing away from the broken glass on the floor. 'Shame.'

On his way out he stood aside for a male customer who looked curiously at Rhiannon and Peri and commented, 'Had an accident?'

Peri said, 'Be careful where you step. We'll have it cleaned up in a jiff.' He looked at Rhiannon. 'You okay?'

'Yes.' *Get a grip.* 'Take those away and bring a brush and pan, would you, please?'

She picked her way through the glass to her place behind the counter.

By the time the customer left, Peri had swept up all the glass. He handed her a small white envelope. 'This was with the flowers.'

She hesitated before she lifted the flap that was tucked into the top and drew out a card bearing a single, bold initial G.

'Oh...' She slumped against the counter.

'My guess is your angel Gabriel,' Peri said. He waited, and when she didn't say any more asked, 'What shall I do with the flowers?'

Her first thought was *Throw them away.* She said, 'You can have them.'

Peri looked dubious. 'You sure about that?'

She opened her mouth to say yes, then hesitated, watching two women enter from the street. 'No,' she said. 'Find a vase and…' she looked around '…somewhere to put it. Maybe our customers will appreciate them.'

Peri smiled. 'Right, boss.' He arranged them in a bulbous china bowl and set them on a plinth inside the window among several artworks.

At just after five Rhiannon looked up from serving a customer and saw Gabriel standing outside, looking at the roses.

He caught her eye through the glass, raised a hand in greeting and came to the door. When the customer had gone he approached the counter. 'You gave my flowers pride of place?' he said.

'Peri did.' He'd put them as far from the counter as he could.

'At least you didn't dump them.'

She felt her eyes widen as her head jerked up. How could he know…?

'Ah…' Gabriel said softly, leaning on the counter. 'You thought about it. I'd hoped you'd got over being angry with me.'

Rhiannon swallowed. Her pulses gradually steadied. 'I'm not angry with you, but…' she breathed in deeply, '…it might be best if we kept to a business relationship in future.' She'd thought it over last night, and in the early hours of the morning had come to a decision.

Gabriel straightened, frowning. 'Why?'

'It's not a good idea to mix business and personal relationships. It's too easy to…to cross the line.'

It had all seemed terribly logical in her mind. Now she was bungling. Making her voice crisp, she said, 'I'm sure you don't make a habit of dating your employees.'

'You're not an employee. You're an independent artist, and we have a contract.'

'Nothing in writing.'

'Verbal agreements are legally binding.'

If they could be proven. But that wasn't what this was really about. 'Going out with you is no part of it.'

'I'll insert a clause,' he said. At her swift recoil, he amended impatiently, 'You know I don't mean that. But aren't you cutting off your nose to spite your face?'

'You have a pretty high opinion of yourself!' Rhiannon shot back, astonished at her own temerity, but experiencing a surge of bitter triumph when a slight colour appeared along his cheekbones.

The triumph faded when he flattened his hands on the counter between them, his expression turning deadly. 'Unless you're a much better actress than I take you for,' he said, 'you were having a thoroughly good time last night. Until I spoiled it for you.'

His stance, looming over her, and the way he was looking at her as though barely containing his temper, didn't help her peace of mind.

Perhaps Gabriel realised it. He straightened again. 'Are you going to let one crass mistake ruin what might be something pretty damn wonderful?'

Was she making a scary mountain out of an insignificant molehill? Aware that she was oversensitive about some things, Rhiannon wavered.

Peri emerged from the back room holding a piece of paper. 'Hi,' he said to Gabriel. 'Excuse me a minute— Rhee, I can't read this address.'

She deciphered it for him, and Gabriel stood back as two people came through the door and began browsing.

When Peri disappeared again, Rhiannon approached the customers, offering information about the pieces they were looking at.

Usually she just greeted people, invited them to look about and ask questions if they wanted any information. She didn't like pushy sales people herself, and anyway felt more comfortable behind the counter. But she needed a breathing space.

Gabriel began to wander unobtrusively—inasmuch as he was ever likely to appear unobtrusive—in the background, until Peri reappeared. Then he picked up one of the coloured glass sculptures that had arrived that morning and started talking to the other man in a low voice.

He was still there when the other customers left empty-handed. After replacing the sculpture on the shelf, he strolled towards her, and Peri busied himself straightening the books on the rear wall.

Rhiannon took up her station again behind the counter. Gabriel came to stand before it, his hands in his pockets. His gaze rested on her almost speculatively. 'Have a drink with me, and we can talk about what's bothering you.'

'I'm sorry, I have things to do.' She'd planned to stay late after closing the gallery. It was time to do her GST return, and the tax department wouldn't wait. That helped to stiffen her resolve.

She was relieved when more last-minute customers breezed in. 'I'll try to get that quote to you within a week or two,' she promised.

Gabriel stepped back. 'Fine. I'll see you again,' he said pleasantly, at last making for the door.

She told herself it wasn't a threat.

*   *   *

Gabriel silently cursed himself as strode away from the gallery, knowing that he'd blundered. The last thing Rhiannon needed was scare tactics. Not that she hadn't stood up to him, with that crack suggesting he was full of himself.

His mouth turned down. Maybe he was over-confident; maybe he'd grown arrogant and self-satisfied. Certainly he'd never had to work so hard at getting close to a woman. Being unaccustomed to rejection, he wasn't sure how to tackle the problem.

But growing angry and exasperated wasn't the way to win Rhiannon's confidence.

Trying to pump Peri hadn't worked either. Obviously the two of them got on well, and an oblique, apparently idle comment to that effect had elicited no information. 'She's a good boss,' Peri said, 'and a good woman.' His hard stare when Gabriel lifted his eyes from seeming absorption in the heavy sculpture in his hand seemed to indicate that Peri would punch the lights out of anybody who suggested differently. Then, out of the blue, he'd added, 'If you want my advice, don't send her any more flowers.'

Gabriel narrowed his eyes. Was he being warned off the grass? Softly he said, 'Would you care to explain that?'

Peri's gaze slid to Rhiannon, apparently deeply engaged with her customers, and he transferred his attention back to Gabriel with an oddly intent look, flexing his splendid shoulders. 'Just take my word for it, mate.'

Gabriel hefted the sculpture he held. When he'd come to fetch Rhiannon before the show she'd been standing close to Peri, his hand touching her hair, and she had been laughing at something he'd said. There'd been warmth in the way she smiled. Gabriel had felt a pang of jealousy, aware that she'd never smiled at him in that way—without the least hint of strain. 'Are we talking dog-in-the-manger here?' he inquired.

Peri scowled. 'Huh? Look, Rhiannon isn't like other women. She's…' He looked over at her again, then back to Gabriel, aggression in his face. 'All I'm saying is, you be careful. Okay?'

Then Rhiannon's customers left and Gabriel headed for her side, but didn't manage to get there before she'd barricaded herself again behind the counter, as if the solid bit of furniture between them was something she needed for protection.

He should have waited until she was closing the gallery, Gabriel told himself, cutting a preoccupied swathe through the home-going throng on the narrow pavement. Only he hadn't been able to wait a moment longer to see her and try to mend the damage of last night. He'd wanted to be on the doorstep first thing this morning, until caution had urged him not to be pushy. The flowers had seemed a good compromise. A silent apology that had often worked in the past. With other women.

Rhiannon isn't like other women. Peri's words re-echoed. Unconsciously scowling, Gabriel almost knocked down a little old lady, and stopped to sincerely apologise as he steadied her with both hands.

'That's quite all right.' The woman twinkled up at him with faded blue eyes. 'My eyesight isn't as good as it used to be.'

'Are you sure you're not hurt?' He felt birdlike shoulder bones under his fingers.

'Not at all. In fact you've made my day. It's a long time since I got so close to a handsome young man.'

His mood momentarily lightening, Gabriel grinned down at her. 'Thank you. But you just said your eyesight isn't so good.'

She chuckled. 'I'm near-sighted. Close up, I can see perfectly. If only I were forty years younger…'

'You must have been a knockout. You still are.'

Her eyes sparkled again. 'You've got a way with you, haven't you? I bet you've got a nice young girlfriend. Lucky woman.'

Watching her retreat along the street, Gabriel wished that Rhiannon shared her opinion. Why couldn't all women be so gracious about accepting an apology?

Admittedly he'd had more to apologise to Rhiannon about. He wondered if it was true she was busy tonight. Or was she punishing him for his transgression?

Almost immediately he dismissed the thought. One thing he was sure of—Rhiannon wasn't one of those women who blew hot and cold just to keep a man on his toes. She didn't even seem to know how to play the kind of games that one or two of his previous lovers had enjoyed—until he grew tired of indulging them and broke off the relationship.

Last night he'd had every intention of kissing her before they parted. A real kiss that would leave her, he hoped, dreaming of him all night and craving more.

That blasted security light with its merciless bulb hadn't helped. But, face it, by then the damage had been thoroughly done anyway. Her mood had switched dramatically in the taxi.

And her anger had been fuelled, he was certain, by fear.

Who had frightened her that much? What had he done to her? And when?

His hands had curled into fists. Deliberately he relaxed them, and fished for his car key. If he could persuade Rhiannon to confide in him she might get over... whatever it was that was inhibiting her natural response.

He sat in his car, staring absently at a concrete wall, his fingers clenched hard on the steering wheel.

She'd said she liked him. He wanted a whole lot more than liking. He wanted passion, a wild, wanton loving. And something told him that despite her repressed exterior and her obvious reluctance to admit to sexual desire, if he could only break through the barriers she protected so fiercely, making love with Rhiannon would be unlike anything he'd known.

He started the car and backed out. A sign fixed to a pillar warned PROCEED WITH CAUTION.

'Good advice,' Gabriel murmured. He'd be wise to take it.

CHAPTER FIVE

RHIANNON stretched stiff muscles, pushing away the completed tax form. Maybe she should get an accountant to do the paperwork. She'd always enjoyed dealing with figures, but there was only so much time in the day, and if it came to a choice she'd prefer to spend more of it on her art.

Which reminded her of her promise to Gabriel.

And of Gabriel himself. He stepped into her memory in vivid colour, big and confident, and too clever for her peace of mind, awakening dormant emotions that until recently she'd found it easier to live without.

She'd been comfortable then, contented and safe, cocooned in the life she'd painstakingly built for herself.

Now she wasn't comfortable anymore. Her equilibrium was askew, and it was all Gabriel Hudson's fault.

The picture of the angel was pinned to the wall over her desk, so she would see it several times a day, helping the creative process.

Maybe that was why it was so difficult to banish his mortal namesake from her thoughts. Inevitably one brought to mind the other.

She stared for a while at the picture, drew a sheet of blank paper towards her and began to draw.

Several hours and a dozen sheets of paper later she returned to the real world.

The traffic noise that hummed all day and most of the

night was strangely missing. The clock over her desk told her she'd worked into the early hours. And she was cold.

But she knew what she wanted to do with the blank wall in the Angelair Building.

Blinking, she reached for the phone, not fancying the car park at this hour, and called a taxi to take her home.

A few hours later her alarm woke her at the usual time and she stumbled out of bed.

Janette, making coffee in the kitchen, gave her a curious glance. 'You were in late. Heavy date?'

'Work,' Rhiannon replied, getting herself a cup. 'Sorry if I woke you.'

'No, I'd just got in myself. Working night and day isn't good for your health, you know. How long since you had a date?'

Janette was good at minding her own business, but there was genuine concern behind her casual air.

'The night before last,' Rhiannon defended herself.

'Oh?' Pouring hot water into a cup, Janette paused. 'Was it good?'

'Yes.' It had been good, until… 'Janette, supposing a man you'd met looked up your address without your knowledge…would it bother you?'

'Hmm.' Janette sat down at the breakfast table and waited for Rhiannon to do the same. 'Depends,' she said judiciously. 'If I really liked him, and he did it to send me flowers or something I'd probably be rather pleased. As long he didn't use it to stalk me or anything like that.'

Rhiannon stirred sugar into her coffee. She shivered, and drank some of the hot liquid to warm herself.

Janette said, 'Are you worried?'

Logic told her that Gabriel Hudson was unlikely to be so desperate. And Janette was an utterly sane, down-to-earth sort of girl, so her opinion held weight. 'No.'

For the rest of that week, every time someone came into the shop after five, Rhiannon looked up with expectant trepidation, but Gabriel didn't appear.

At the weekend she finished the church commission and had no excuse to keep relegating Gabriel and his project to the back of her mind. Or at least pretending to.

During the following week she did a final sketch plan of her proposal for the mosaic wall, and over the next weekend she visited several suppliers.

By Monday she'd drawn up a pricing plan, and while Peri dealt with customers, she sat at her desk staring at the phone for several minutes, braced herself and picked it up.

When she was put through to Gabriel she had to take a deep breath. 'I have a final design for you,' she told him, 'and a price,' quickly rattling it off.

He didn't respond immediately, and she said, 'I know it sounds a lot, but it's not over-expensive for—'

'It's a fair price,' he interrupted. 'I won't quibble about it. But I'd like to see the finished design before we agree on a contract.'

'Of course. I was going to suggest that.'

'If you don't want to leave the gallery I can come to you. Is eleven-thirty a good time?'

In business hours. 'Yes,' she said, feeling oddly blank. She'd frozen him off and he was adhering to her ex-

pressed desire to keep their relationship strictly professional. She ought to be pleased.

'I'll be there.'

Almost brusque, Rhiannon thought as she put the
phone down and realised that her palms were damp,
leaving a fading bloom on the plastic. She took a tissue
from a box on the desk and wiped them, trying to dis-
miss a sense of dismay.

Gabriel put down the phone and scowled at it, idly turning a ballpoint pen end over end against the open appointments diary his secretary had placed on his desk.

His impulse had been to go round to the gallery right
away. The same impulse he'd fought all last week. But
pragmatism intervened. At eleven-thirty there was a
chance he could persuade Rhiannon to have lunch with
him. A business lunch, he'd tell her. If he could find
something in the design or the contract to cavil over,
that might work...

Unless she used it as an excuse to withdraw from the
project. His hand stilled.

He was pretty sure she was committed to the mosaic,
excited about it. It was his trump card. Once he had the
contract in his pocket she couldn't completely withdraw
from his life until that was done. And he'd keep a very
good eye on progress—she'd agreed he could watch her
work.

That was something to look forward to.

He was deliberately fifteen minutes late for their ap-
pointment, armed with apologies about a fictitious meeting that had run overtime. There were several people in

the gallery, and he had to wait another few minutes for Rhiannon to be free.

She brushed aside his excuse. 'You'd better come out the back,' she said, leading him through the door.

As she crossed to a desk in one corner Gabriel took a swift inventory of the room. Bigger than he'd have expected, but very much a work and storage space, giving little hint of anything personal.

'This is the design.' Rhiannon laid a large sheet of heavy paper onto a wide work counter. 'I hope you approve.'

He came to her side, holding one side of the paper against its tendency to curl, while she anchored the other.

The colours echoed the Internet picture she'd shown him, and although the effect was abstract, there was a surreal suggestion of the angel's robes and silver wings, even on closer inspection a face, and long, streaming golden hair merging into the rest of the design. That and a streak of silver running right across the page were suggestive of speed and light.

'You can do this in mosaic?' he queried.

'Yes. But the silver bits will be overpainted with metallic paint. I thought of mirror glass instead, but paint will give a softer effect, in keeping with the other colours. Do you like it?'

Remembering his plan, he said, 'Can you explain some of the symbolism?'

He'd thought he didn't really need it, but she showed him things he hadn't noticed, although half the time he was watching the unusual animation in Rhiannon's face instead of following the finger she used to trace the various elements.

She straightened, tucking a strand of hair behind her ear, her eyes alight and her expression for once unguarded when she faced him, so beautiful he felt as if an unseen hand gripped his heart. A sensation of purest pleasure seared him.

Something must have shown in his expression. He saw her eyes widen, the pupils enlarge, and her lips momentarily parted, waking a terrible urge in him to close them with his own. Then she blinked and took a step back. Her hand released the drawing and the paper curled into a loose roll.

She raised a hand unnecessarily to her hair again, and gave a small nervous laugh. 'That's it,' she said. 'I hope it's what you want.'

Realising she was still waiting for his verdict, and unable to pretend there was a thing wrong with the proposal, he said, 'It's brilliant. Exactly what I want—no, it's more than I ever hoped for.'

Rhiannon relaxed a little. Even smiled, though it was a slightly guarded, strained smile. 'If you're satisfied, I've made two copies of a contract.' She turned away from him to the desk, pulling out a drawer.

Damned if he was satisfied. He wouldn't be satisfied until he had her in his bed, where he'd teach her what satisfaction was all about. He wanted to see that absorbed animation in her face when she looked at him— see it directed at him instead of a work of art. Wanted to watch it change to a taut mask of desire that disintegrated into the uncontrollable, naked delight of sexual fulfilment.

She bent and pulled out a couple of sheets of paper from the drawer, and Gabriel, admiring the curve of her behind where her skirt tightened over it, allowed himself a moment of fantasy.

'If you want any changes…' she was saying, turning to him.

Her face did go taut then, but not with desire—it looked more like apprehension. Guiltily, Gabriel transferred his attention to the contract she held, hiding his eyes behind lowered lids. He made a thing of consulting his watch. 'Why don't we discuss that over a business lunch?'

Rhiannon told herself she'd been mistaken. Gabriel Hudson wasn't the sort of man who eyed a woman like a tiger sizing up its prey. The suggestion of lunch was made in the tone of a man who had little time to waste and proposed combining the necessary act of eating with the business at hand. And when he looked at her again his eyes were cool and expressionless.

'We often get busy over lunchtime,' she said. 'I don't want to leave Peri to cope on his own.'

His eyelids flickered infinitesimally, the only reaction she could discern, then his gaze went beyond her and she realised Peri had entered the room as she spoke.

'No problem, boss,' Peri said cheerfully. 'Don't you trust me?'

'Of course I trust you!'

'Then go for it,' he advised airily. 'I can manage okay.'

Gabriel raised his brows at Rhiannon. 'Shall we?'

He indicated the door, and Peri said, waving a piece of paper, 'I have an order for another of those brass candlesticks we had last month. I'll leave it on your desk, okay? See you later then,' he added firmly.

'I suppose,' Rhiannon conceded, 'I could spare half an hour.' Picking up her bag, she put the contract copies into it.

At a nearby café-bar that was spacious and not yet too crowded, a waitress showed them to a corner table near a window. Gabriel removed his jacket and slung it over the back of his chair before sitting down and giving their order.

Rhiannon handed over the contracts. He read a copy quickly and asked two questions that she answered apparently satisfactorily, then he scrawled a signature at the bottom of each copy. 'I'll make sure you get the first-stage cheque as per the agreement by tomorrow,' he promised.

'Thanks. I'll need that to buy the materials.'

He pushed the papers over to her and offered her the handsome, gold-trimmed pen he'd signed with, warm from his fingers, to add her own neat signature.

Gabriel seemed to study it for a moment before taking his copy and tucking it into his breast pocket. Rhiannon passed back the pen and he put that away, then held out his hand. 'Shake on it?'

She allowed him to fold her hand in his, and he retained it for a second before releasing her.

As the waitress brought their order he asked Rhiannon, 'When *can* you start on the mural? I'll order that scaffolding for you.'

'I'll let you know. It depends on how quickly I can get the materials together.' She returned her own copy of the contract to her bag. 'Do you have some place where they could be stored in the building? The tiles will need quite a bit of room.'

'I'll find somewhere. It needs to be close to the site, I suppose.'

'If possible.'

'I'll make it possible,' Gabriel said.

She edged a glance at him as she began cutting her salad-stuffed croissant in half, and he said, 'If you want it enough, anything's possible.'

'No—' The knife in Rhiannon's hand slipped and cut painfully into her thumb. She dropped the knife onto her plate and lifted her thumb to her mouth.

Gabriel reached out and pulled her hand away, gripping her wrist to inspect the thin pink line on her skin.

'It's nothing,' Rhiannon said, as the pink line turned red with blood. 'The knife isn't even sharp.'

'Sharp enough.' He picked up a paper napkin, folded it into a pad and pressed it over the tiny wound.

'Really,' Rhiannon said shakily, 'it's not worth fussing over.'

She made to withdraw her hand but he only said, 'Keep still and the bleeding will stop a lot quicker.'

'I'm not usually accident-prone.' This was the second time she'd done something silly while eating with Gabriel. 'You must think I'm an idiot.' At least he hadn't been there to see her smash glass all over the floor when he sent her flowers.

He smiled. 'I know you're not. You're a savvy businesswoman and a gifted artist. Quite a combination.'

'Not all artists have their heads in the clouds.' If they kept talking maybe she could distract her mind from the fact that his hand wrapped her wrist, warming the skin and making her pulse jump about, and that his other hand cradled hers while his thumb exerted pressure on the makeshift first-aid pad.

'Obviously. What did you mean, no?'

Rhiannon's throat tightened. If he hadn't been holding her so firmly her hand would have jerked. 'I…don't remember what we were talking about.'

'I said a person can get anything if they want it badly enough, and you said…*No.*'

Her gaze was on their hands. She moistened her lips briefly with her tongue and, keeping her voice steady, said, 'It doesn't always work that way. Not if what you want depends on some other person wanting it too, just as much.'

An inclination of his head conceded the point. 'There's such a thing as compromise. Whenever possible I try to bring about a win-win situation for all concerned.'

'Sometimes,' Rhiannon said, staring so hard at the folded white napkin that her eyes stung, 'someone has to lose.'

He said, 'I'm not a loser.' As a chill attacked her spine, he added, 'And neither are you.'

That brought her eyes to his. His gaze was calm and steady, the light through the window accentuating the silvery look she'd come to associate with him.

She said, 'I think it's stopped bleeding.'

Carefully he lifted a corner of the napkin and peeked, then very gently peeled it away, releasing her hand. 'No lasting damage.'

'No,' she said. Wounds healed. Scars faded into insignificance with time. Miracles happened. Even physically disabled people sometimes astonished the medical world.

There was curiosity in his gaze. 'What are you thinking?'

Rhiannon shook her head. 'Nothing.' She picked up the croissant and bit into it, an excuse not to talk. Nothing she could tell him. Nothing she could tell anybody until she'd conquered the dark demons of her past.

Gabriel sawed a piece off his superburger. Of course she wasn't going to explain to him what had brought that sudden determination to her face, the spark in her green eyes like a light of battle, followed by a Mona Lisa smile.

Rhiannon was an expert at guarding her thoughts, giving nothing away of her inner self if she could help it. Fortunately she wasn't always able to hide her feelings. He was learning to read them in her face—something that she'd probably find unwelcome. But as for asking her point-blank to reveal them—he should have known better. Because now she was climbing back into her shell with the pretence of eating.

'How's the croissant?' he asked, for want of something better to break the silence.

'Fine. And your lunch?' Glancing at what was left of his burger.

He hadn't even tasted it, shovelling food in his mouth while all his attention concentrated on every tiny nuance of Rhiannon's expression, her voice.

Her pulse under his had been erratic, he'd noted. Because he was holding her hand, or because the small accident had affected her? Some people couldn't stand

the sight of blood, even the tiniest amount. 'Good,' he
answered. The burger had been large, anyway, and the
potato chips with it were crisp. Before she could fill her
mouth again, he dredged up, 'I'll arrange a key card for
the building for you, since you'll be working on the
mural after business hours when everyone else is gone.'

'Oh…thanks.'

Detecting a note of reserve, he said, 'A custodian lives
on the top floor and has an office in the basement. If
you have any problems you can call on him.'

'I will.' Was that relief that flitted across her face?
Maybe she was nervous of being in the deserted building
alone. If so, he had a hunch she wouldn't admit to it.

She picked up her croissant again and he couldn't see
her expression anymore.

At the next table a party of twenty-something suit-
wearing males, their cell phones on the table vying for
whose was the smallest, was growing raucous as the men
exchanged banter with a waitress. Gabriel threw an ir-
ritated glance in their direction.

Rhiannon finished the croissant and emptied her coffee cup, then checked her watch and got up. 'I have to
go.'

Reluctantly Gabriel pushed away his empty plate and
stood, too, pausing to retrieve his jacket from the back
of the chair.

Their neighbours had commandeered a couple of extra
chairs and one of the young men, sporting a carefully
trimmed Van Dyke beard on a flabby chin, had pushed
himself back to stretch his legs under the table, blocking
the way out.

'Excuse me,' Rhiannon said.

The man looked up, slowly taking in the whole of her body on the way to her face. Then he leered. 'Sure, babe.'

He didn't immediately move, taking his damn time and obviously enjoying the moment while his grinning companions looked on. Gabriel moved forward, his hand going to Rhiannon's waist as he glared over her shoulder at the lout.

The man's gaze shifted to him and he blinked, then straightened and stood up, pulling the chair out of the way and giving them an exaggerated bow as they passed. The others laughed.

'Smart-ar…aleck,' Gabriel muttered as he and Rhiannon stepped into the street. He realised she was trembling, and pulled her closer to his side before re-membering that probably wasn't the cleverest thing to do, and loosening his hold. 'Are you all right?'

'Of course.' Predictably, she extricated herself from his arm. 'It was nothing. He was just being stupid.'

Normally Gabriel would have dismissed the incident as trivial, not been consumed by a murderous desire to wipe the smirk off the idiot's baby face with a well-placed punch.

Women were subjected to that sort of thing all the time. Most of them shrugged off the offensive behaviour as annoying but nothing to get worked up about. Some might even have laughed, or put the man down with a basilisk stare. Gabriel knew a few who were capable of that.

It might have been a minor incident, but it was symp-tomatic of an attitude that had never really made him angry before. Perhaps it should have.

No man had a right to bully a woman—and bullying was what that café Romeo had been doing. He'd enjoyed trapping Rhiannon, embarrassing her, prolonging her discomfort until he was forced to adopt some semblance of civilised behaviour.

Whatever it was that lay in Rhiannon's past had made that sort of thing not at all minor for her.

He could find out—even if it meant hiring someone to dig into her life. He'd used an agency several times to conduct checks on people who wanted to work for him, even once or twice on dodgy clients. It was sensible business practice, to protect his company. But, damn, he couldn't do that to Rhiannon. He'd made her a promise. The revelation had to come from her.

Would she ever trust him enough to tell him?

CHAPTER SIX

RHIANNON sent Peri off for a quick lunch of his own and tried to concentrate on making shelf labels instead of thinking about Gabriel Hudson.

She'd been almost prepared to forgive his intrusion into her privacy, perhaps tell him she realised she'd overreacted.

The right moment hadn't seemed to arise, and then that incident as they left the café had rocked her equilibrium. She'd been grateful for his strong presence at her back, and in the street, when he'd pulled her closer to him, the temptation to accept the comfort of his arms endangered the fragile control that prevented her inward quaking from becoming visible.

He'd have thought she was nuts, going to pieces over something so petty.

Carefully lettering a sign while looking up now and then to keep an eye on a couple of browsers, she paused, calligraphy pen in hand, the letters before her eyes blurring. She'd coped with similar situations before, and not fallen apart afterwards. Not lately anyway. In a public place, she'd been perfectly safe from any real assault. The man had been teasing, that was all, showing off. The waitress hadn't seemed to mind the group's behaviour.

But the urge to collapse against Gabriel, simply because he'd seemed to intuitively understand her revulsion, was disturbing.

And dangerous. Rhiannon had learned the hard way to rely on no one but herself, to stand on her own feet, manage her own problems. She wasn't about to compromise that—it was an autonomy that had been too hard-won.

Somehow Gabriel had infiltrated her defences—defences that she needed to function in the world. Feelings, emotions that she'd thought shut away for ever had surfaced in his company. Some of them were good feelings, if a little nerve-racking. Before discovering he'd found out her home address, she'd been tentatively moving towards exploring them, giving them room to grow and develop into—maybe—something deeper.

But if it meant she was opening the door to other vulnerable emotions...

She couldn't afford that at the expense of all she had regained over the last five years.

Gabriel's caring protectiveness had the potential to undermine her determined independence. It was a snare and a temptation, because if she allowed herself to be seduced by it, to depend on his strength, and then it was taken away...

She'd be thrust right back into the black pit of despair that she'd so determinedly clawed her way out of. Twice.

'Excuse me?'

The impatient voice intruded on her thoughts, and she looked up to see a woman at the other side of the counter clutching a small painting. 'I said, how much is this? I can't read the price here.'

'I'm sorry.' Rhiannon took the picture and turned it over, reading out the price. She must remember to make her figures larger. Her writing was naturally small.

Peri breezed back in, holding the door for the customer as she left clutching her painting. The other browsers had gone without buying, and he asked Rhiannon, 'And how was *your* lunch?'

'We signed a contract for his mural,' she said repressively.

'It can't have been all business.'

'Yes, it was.' Rhiannon returned to her lettering. 'Don't you have some unpacking to do? I think there's room on that shelf in the corner. You can shift some of the ceramic pieces to the floor.'

'Sure, boss.' He gave her a little salute and a penetrating look before swaggering off to the workroom.

Rhiannon sighed. She hadn't meant to be sharp with Peri. It wasn't his fault she was unsettled and unsure. To be fair, she supposed it wasn't Gabriel's fault either.

No, the trouble was in her.

And that, she thought with a surge of anger that shook her from head to toe, wasn't her fault either. One thing all those months of counselling had done was convince her of that—and finally that she was the only one who could effect a cure.

She finished the card she was working on and picked up another, deliberately making bolder strokes with the pen, the lettering larger.

Tomorrow she'd start ordering supplies for the Angelair mosaic. She'd have to phone Gabriel and check on that storage space he'd promised.

The thought brought a range of complicated emotions. Anxiety, hope, and anticipation. None of them logical.

And none of them necessary, as it turned out. While she procrastinated, arguing that he'd hardly have had time to make any arrangements, he phoned her the following morning.

'We have a basement room for you,' he said. 'It's near the rear elevators so your materials can be taken up as you need them. I'll make sure someone is around to help with any lifting and carrying.'

'I don't think that's really necessary.'

'I do. I know how heavy those tiles are, remember?'

She did remember, vividly, how easily he'd carried a box full of them for her after she'd made a fool of herself by dropping them at his feet.

'I won't need tiles for a while yet,' she told him. 'Not until I've done the cartoon.'

'The what?'

'A coloured sketch on the wall, to guide me.' For most projects she'd have worked on backing panels in her studio, fixing them in place later, but this was so big and complex she had decided it was better to do it in situ rather than risk the pieces not fitting together perfectly.

'Uh-huh. I've contacted a scaffolder,' Gabriel told her. 'When you need it you can come along and make sure it's what you want.'

The scaffolding was erected on a Friday after the building had closed.

Gabriel watched closely as the team worked to Rhiannon's direction, and inspected the result afterwards, testing various joints and bits of piping to ensure they were secure.

'I'm sure it's all right,' Rhiannon assured him.

'You're not nervous about working up there?'

'Not specially.' A tumble down the stairs could be disastrous, but the sturdy safety rail he'd insisted on should save her from that. 'I'll be fine.'

'This light isn't great,' Gabriel remarked critically, looking up at the contemporary chandelier hanging overhead. 'If you plan to work at night you'll need some spotlights or something. I'll see what I can do.'

'Thank you.' Taking a large sheet of paper from the cylinder tucked under her arm, she rolled the design back the other way to straighten it, then opened it out, studying the gridlines she'd drawn.

'Is that to scale?' Gabriel asked.

'Yes—I don't want to make any mistakes on something this size. I'll draw a grid on the wall first.'

'Can I be of any help?'

She'd been going to ask Peri, offering to pay him, but felt guilty about taking him away from his own art. His time was already severely limited by his job at the gallery.

When she hesitated Gabriel added, 'I said I wouldn't hurry you, but there are safety issues as long as the scaffolding is in place. If there's an emergency and we can't use the elevators we'd have major problems with an obstructed stairway.'

That was a point. There was still room for a person to pass the scaffolding, but it had certainly limited the space. 'I'll complete the top half first, and then the scaffolding can come down.'

'When do you plan to start?'

'Tomorrow after the gallery closes I have a few hours.'

'I'll be here. But this is your key card for future use.' He dug in his pocket and handed her an envelope. 'I'll show you how to use it.'

As they descended the stairs a burly middle-aged man in uniform appeared in the lobby, and Gabriel introduced him as the custodian.

Mick Dysart shook Rhiannon's hand with a large paw and assured her he'd be available whenever she wanted him. 'If I'm not in my office downstairs,' he said, 'there's a buzzer on the wall near the lifts, and another one at the staff door. Just use that and I'll be with you in a jiff.'

Escorting her to her car, Gabriel said, 'If you're leaving after dark anytime I'm not around, Mick or one of security guards that cover his time off will make sure you get safely to your car, or call a taxi for you.'

When she arrived on Saturday afternoon he was already on the landing, looking up at the wall. Two large floodlights on tall stands stood there, too, electric cables snaking around them and disappearing up the stairwell.

'Have you had something to eat?' he asked her.

'Yes.' She'd snacked on sandwiches and coffee before leaving the gallery.

They worked out a system for drawing the grid, and between the two of them finished it by the time darkness began to fall outside. 'Thank you,' she said, easing her back against her hands after descending from the scaffolding. 'I didn't expect to get it all done today.'

'What's next?'

'I'll transfer the drawing to the wall.'

'I suppose that's something you'll need to do on your own.'

'Yes. But I appreciate this.'

'Can I offer you a meal?'

'I'm having dinner with friends tonight.' She was glad of a valid excuse, suppressing a pang of regret. 'And you don't need to feed me.'

'As long as someone does.'

On Sunday she'd been working for half an hour, sketching the first outlines on the wall, when she heard footsteps on the marble floor. Pausing, she looked down from her perch on the scaffolding, expecting to see the custodian. Instead Gabriel stood at the bottom of the stairs, one hand on the baluster.

He said, 'I thought you might be here.'

'I didn't think you would be.' Their voices sounded eerily hushed in the empty building. It was quieter than yesterday, when the demolition team had been working next door, and the muffled sounds of jackhammers and machines had penetrated the walls.

'I have some paperwork to catch up on. I hope you don't mean to stick at that all day. Six days in the gallery and spending the rest of the weekend working for me is slave labour and I won't have it.'

'This is different from the gallery.'

'A labour of love?' His mouth curved.

'I know I'm getting paid for it, but it's what I love to do, yes.'

'Well, don't stay too long. Do you need anything?'

Rhiannon shook her head. 'No. Thanks,' she added.

He stood there a moment longer. 'Okay. See you, then.'

Listening to him walk away, she remained as she was for several seconds, the carpenter's pencil held in her slack hand. He'd gone, just like that.

Returning to the drawing, she made a mistake and swore under her breath.

The custodian checked on her a couple of times, watching for a while, then wandered off again. At one o'clock Gabriel reappeared. 'Have you had lunch?' he demanded from the bottom of the stairs. 'A break?'

'Yes I have.' She'd brought sandwiches and fruit and eaten them sitting on the stairs. 'I told you not to worry about me.'

'This is a big job for one person.'

'I can do it.'

'I wasn't implying you can't. But I don't want to see you work yourself into the ground.'

'You won't. I can look after myself.' She'd been do-ing it for long enough.

He looked at his watch. 'I have to go. Mick will be around if you need anything.'

On Monday Gabriel stopped by for a little longer before leaving the building. She had to force herself to concen-trate while he watched, and only relaxed again when he said goodnight.

At eight o'clock Mick offered her a coffee, and brought it to her, then sat alongside her on the stairs and chatted while she drank it.

He told her he was widowed and had two daughters

about her age, one married. 'These are my grandkids,' he said, showing her a photograph of three smiling children with their mother. 'Pity the wife didn't live to see them.'

'They're lovely,' Rhiannon said. She liked children— they were unthreatening and fun, although of course they also entailed pretty heavy responsibilities for parents, as she'd realised from being around her friends' families. In a vague way she'd hoped one day she'd have some of her own. But she'd blocked from her mind all consideration of the necessary preliminaries.

Each evening Rhiannon drove her car close to the Angelair Building, taking advantage of the emptying spaces during the homeward rush hour. On Friday, she buzzed at the staff door on leaving, and a few minutes later, instead of Mick, Gabriel himself came down the stairs, looking more handsome than ever in an open-collared white shirt, the sleeves carelessly rolled, and dark pants.

'You're working late,' she said.

'Ditto,' he replied, opening the door. 'How's it going? It looked this morning as if you were close to finishing the drawing.'

'I have now. Tomorrow I'll start painting in the colours.' They began walking towards her car.

'You'll want some help lugging paint cans. I'll come in.'

'You said Mick would help.'

'Mick's having the weekend off to see his family.'

'Don't *you* ever have time off?'

'I'm the boss. I take it when I can.'

Not when he might have liked to, Rhiannon noted. When he could. Working long hours was probably a habit he'd developed young, one that had helped to make his business what it was today.

'What time do you plan to arrive?' he asked.

'About two thirty, after I've finished at the gallery.'

'I'll be here.'

When they reached the car and she took out the key he leaned against the rear side window, arms folded, while she inserted the key in the lock.

'You told me once,' he said, 'that you liked me. Has that changed?'

'No,' she said, before remembering the context— when he kissed her in his office. Of course she didn't dislike him. She was just distrustful of the effect he had on her.

Next day, Gabriel met her dressed in jeans and a T-shirt, helped her put down a heavy drop sheet, and carried paint cans up from the basement.

As she began brushing on the first strokes of blue background he said, 'It's a bit light, isn't it?'

'These colours are only approximate,' she assured him, 'watered down. Just a guide for the tesserae.'

'Uh-huh. So…could I do some of that?'

It would be less nerve-racking than having him stand and watch, as he was now, his arms folded, legs apart as if studying her technique. 'I suppose so,' she said after a moment's thought. 'If you start on the high point at the other end we could meet in the middle.'

He slanted a grin at her. 'Sounds like a good idea.'

When they did, she stepped back along the trestle they stood on and let him finish the last bit of blue.

'How did I do?' he asked her.

'Not bad.' He looked rather pleased with himself, and she laughed. 'You can do some more if you like.' She'd almost begun to get used to his presence, silently working under her instructions, filling in the larger blocks of colour while she dealt with the fiddly bits.

At five he said, 'You're not planning to work much longer, I hope?'

Rhiannon shook her head. 'I'm having a meal with some friends tonight.'

'I've been invited to check out a new night club next Saturday. Would you like to come with me?'

The few times she'd visited clubs with a group of women friends it had been more of an ordeal than a pleasurable experience. 'I don't dance,' she told him. 'And we agreed that it's better to keep things on a business footing.'

'Actually, I don't remember agreeing to anything.'

Rhiannon shot him a startled glance.

'Why don't you dance?'

'I'm not very good at it.'

'Practice helps…as in most things.'

'I'm really not very interested.'

His look was penetrating, then he gave a short, harsh laugh. 'You don't know what you're missing.'

The following morning he was waiting for her again, the paint and brushes standing ready while he surveyed what they'd done the night before.

She paused at the foot of the stairs before slowly ascending when he turned to her and said, 'Good morning.'

He didn't remove his gaze from her, seeming to take note of every movement as she came towards him, his expression unreadable but disturbing all the same. His eyes were half closed and glittery.

Rhiannon tried to quell the tug of sexual awareness she'd come to recognise. Awareness so powerful that even though she stood a deliberate few feet away when she reached the landing she could feel her skin tingling, a liquid warmth running along her bones.

He didn't move, standing before the paint pots, and she realised she would have to approach him to reach them.

Her step faltered as she brushed by him, her bare arm coming in contact with the rolled sleeve of the open-necked shirt he wore with his jeans. He still didn't move, and she felt the fine hairs at her nape rise with tension as she knelt to open a paint pot. Her hand was unsteady on the screwdriver she slid under the edge of the lid to lever it up.

Then he was beside her, very close. She felt his body warmth at her shoulder, and his breath stirred a tendril of hair at her temple.

The screwdriver slipped from her hand, landing with a soft clatter on the drip sheet.

Gabriel picked it up, closing his strong fingers around the yellow plastic handle. He took over the task and gave the screwdriver a quick twist, flipping open the lid and catching it before laying it carefully down.

'Thank you,' she said almost inaudibly.

'No problem. Tell me what you want me to do.'

They worked largely in silence, but gradually Rhiannon felt the tension leach away. By the time Mick stopped by and offered to fetch them coffee she was almost back to normal. As normal as she ever was around Gabriel.

At midday Gabriel suggested, 'There's a good restaurant practically next door.'

Rhiannon shook her head. 'I've brought my lunch. You please yourself.'

He left for a while and came back with a pie and a doughnut, and two coffees.

'Thanks,' Rhiannon said when he handed her one of the cups. She sat on the top step, her shoulder wedged against the stair rail while she ate her sandwiches.

Gabriel gave her a thoughtful look and followed suit at the other side of the wide stair, half turned to face her as they sipped the drinks.

'Are you happy,' he asked her, 'with the way things are going?'

Deciding not to read any hidden meaning into that, Rhiannon looked over her shoulder at the cartoon. 'It's coming along faster than I expected, thanks to your help.'

'I'm glad to do it. You know you can call on me any time. For anything.'

She cast him a covert glance, her eyelashes flickering. Temptation beckoned, and she struggled with it before pushing it away. 'I suppose the mosaic will mean all the more to you since you've had a hand in creating it.'

He looked at what they'd done, then back at her. 'This is certainly something to remember.'

By five o'clock a good part of the top half was done,

and Rhiannon climbed down to inspect their handiwork from the ground, easing her back against her hands.

Gabriel followed, standing behind her. 'Enough for today,' he suggested. 'Should we put away the paint and brushes?'

'Mm, I guess.'

'I'll take care of it,' he said, 'after I've seen you out. You need to rest.'

Rhiannon got used to Gabriel's presence and his occasional help. When he wasn't there Mick would stop by to bring her coffee, and see her off the premises at a reasonable hour.

The cartoon done, Rhiannon mixed her mortar with adhesive while Gabriel and Mick fetched and carried for her, hoisting the bucket of mortar and a plastic bin filled with ceramic pieces onto the scaffolding where she could easily reach them.

Mick left, and Rhiannon trowelled some mortar onto the wall, picked out a triangle of blue tile, and carefully placed it. Gabriel stood below her with his hands on his hips, his head tilted.

After adding several more tesserae and with the next in her hand, she looked down at the things she'd left on the drip sheet.

'What do you want?'

She pointed. 'I forgot to bring my tile nippers up here.'

He handed the plier-like tool to her and watched her pull on the safety glasses slung about her neck before closing the tool over the shard of blue, cutting it to the shape she wanted. She pressed it onto the mortar, and then smoothed more of the muddy-looking stuff on a patch of the wall. 'If you have things to do,' she hinted to Gabriel, 'I don't need you now.'

'So you say.' He walked around to look up at her face. 'Am I bothering you?'

After all the helpful stuff he'd done it seemed rude to say so. Rhiannon shrugged. 'It's going to get pretty tedious.'

He folded his arms, standing feet-apart below her. 'I'm not bored yet.'

She turned to pick another fragment from the bin. 'Please yourself.'

'I am. Or at least you're pleasing me.'

Rhiannon couldn't stop her head whipping round, but he was staring with bland appraisal at the wall. 'Looking good.'

That was a bit close to the wind, Gabriel chided himself as Rhiannon returned her attention to her work. He had a lot of ground to make up since she'd backed off after that debacle with the address business. Not that he had any intention of going along forever with this farce of sticking to an impersonal relationship, but neither did he want to make her feel threatened in any way. That would be counter-productive.

'I'll be in my office,' he said, 'for a while. And Mick's around if you need him.'

While he sat hunched over his computer, staring at meaningless figures, he kept thinking of Rhiannon's lithe grace as she bent to find another tessera to add to the design, unconsciously accentuating the curve of her waist and hip; the serene concentration on her face as she chose just the right shape and deftly fitted it into a space; the way she used her slender wrist to restrain an intrusive strand of her hair because her gloved hands were grimed with mortar.

He ached to slam out of the room, race down the stairs and pull her from her perch on the scaffolding, sweep her off to some private corner of the building—he looked at the two sofas in the corner of the room, too damnably small for what he had in mind—and make mad, passionate love to her for the rest of the night…maybe for the rest of their lives.

But she'd rebuffed his carefully casual invitation, and it was no use even thinking about a long-term relationship with a woman who steadfastly, unequivocally refused to allow any romantic overtures.

Well, he wouldn't think about it yet. One step at a time, and who knew how far that might eventually take them?

Gabriel Hudson wasn't a man who easily admitted defeat.

Putting his latest plan into practice, he adopted a laid-back manner and took things slowly. Even when Rhiannon didn't need help he lingered sometimes to watch her work—at first briefly, and then for longer periods as she seemed to accept his presence—and kept scrupulously to his resolution of not pressuring her in the slightest.

Sometimes he deliberately stayed away, hoping she might miss him a little. When he was with her he clamped his tongue, avoiding any provocative remarks, and tried to hide the desire in his eyes. He limited his touch to the occasional light guidance on her arm, and was rewarded by seeing her gradually relax with him.

Schooling his body to emulate the asexual being he'd been named for was torture, yet on some level he gained a novel pleasure from a deepening relationship unlike any he'd known.

It was like watching the unfurling of a tightly folded bud. Every time she smiled, even looked at him openly without veiling her expression or turning away, it contracted his heart.

Sometimes they talked, seldom about personal things, but occasionally he learned something about her childhood, or her relationship with her parents and her grandmother. She'd been happy, he gathered, until the tragedy that had taken her mother and left her father only a shell of the man he had been. Touching on that time made her clam up and he learned to keep away from it.

The day he made her laugh unconstrainedly with some mordantly humorous remark, he felt an adrenaline surge that was almost like sex.

When one evening she voluntarily sat beside him on the stairs to drink coffee that Mick brought them, not so close that they touched, but only inches from him, he counted it as a victory.

Rhiannon scraped out the last of the mortar in the container beside her, buttered a triangular piece of tile with the mixture, and carefully pressed the tessera into place.

Putting down the trowel, she stretched, releasing cramped muscles, and climbed down, doing a few more stretches on the landing. She needed to mix another batch of mortar, but first she made for the water cooler on the ground floor, drank thirstily and splashed her face.

About to climb the stairs again, she looked up at the work she'd done, feeling a certain satisfaction. Of course there was a long way to go but she'd outlined the major features down to the scaffolding and begun filling them in. The higher corner was the most difficult part, reaching up from the scaffolding to place each piece. She still had to finish that.

She massaged a stiffness in her right shoulder. Then jumped as a hand descended on it, replacing hers.

'Sorry,' Gabriel said. 'Didn't you know I was here?'

'I didn't hear you.' He was wearing sneakers and she'd been too preoccupied to notice his approach.

His hand was still on her shoulder, and he began kneading it, then both of them. His fingers were strong and seemingly impersonal. 'Does this help? Tell me if you want me to stop.'

Rhiannon could feel the muscles loosening. She stood under his hands, surprised at her own willingness to submit to his touch. 'I think it helps,' she admitted.

He gave a satisfied little grunt and continued the rhythmic movements.

'Better?' he asked when finally his hands ceased their movement, to rest lightly on her shoulders.

'Thank you.'

'Maybe you've done enough for today.'

'I want to finish that top corner,' she said, gazing up at it. 'I was just about to mix some more mortar.'

'It's high.'

'That's why my shoulder's a bit stiff.'

'Can't I help? If you tell me what to do, it's an easy reach for me.'

'Well…I suppose if I did the buttering and handed the tesserae to you…' It had been more tiring than she'd expected, and more difficult. She didn't want to end up with a repetitive strain injury.

They stood side by side on the scaffolding, Rhiannon gauging what pieces were needed and picking them out, telling Gabriel where to put them. He caught on quite quickly, and in what seemed no time the tricky corner was done.

'The rest will be easier,' Rhiannon said with relief. 'I haven't done anything quite like this before.'

'You're not sorry you took it on?'

'Of course not. It's a great opportunity.'

'One you weren't afraid to take.'

'No.' She shot him a glance before moving away to clean her trowel. Looking at her watch, she was surprised at how late it was. 'Can I leave all this overnight…?' she indicated the tools and materials on the boards '…since tomorrow's Sunday?'

'Sure. Leave everything until tomorrow…or as long as you need.'

Struck by his tone, Rhiannon looked at him again, finding his gaze fixed on her. Then he smiled and, going to the end of the scaffolding, leapt to the floor, straightened easily and held out his arms to her.

'I prefer the safe way,' she said, shaking her head, and opted for climbing down. He put a hand on one of the bars as if to steady it.

'You would have been safe,' he told her when she

reached the floor. His eyes were smiling, although his mouth remained grave. 'I'd have caught you.'

'I know.' She stepped back, wrapping her arms about herself.

'And let you go,' he said slowly, 'if that's what you wanted.'

Rhiannon wasn't sure it would have been what she wanted. Which was a shock in itself. She turned her head to stare blindly at the colours on the wall. *Coward,* an inner voice mocked her.

She forced herself to look at him. He hadn't moved. 'I know,' she repeated, her voice husky.

He waited for a moment as if debating whether to say what was in his mind, before he asked quietly, 'Then what are you afraid of, Rhiannon?'

Rhiannon's teeth bit into her lower lip. *A lot of things.* 'Not of you,' she said, and something flashed in his eyes before he narrowed them, veiling whatever emotion was responsible. 'I know you wouldn't hurt me.' The truth, and it should have been liberating. But... 'It's complicated,' she said lamely.

'Too complicated to tell me about?' His hand shifted slightly on the steel bar he clutched, drawing her eyes. His knuckles had turned almost white.

She brought her gaze back to his face. He was looking at her as if willing her to confide in him. As if it was important to him.

'When I was seventeen,' she said, almost whispering, 'something...happened to me.'

'I know,' he said, and as her heart lurched and she tensed, her stomach churning, he dropped his hand from the scaffolding. 'I mean, I guessed you'd had a bad experience. I didn't know what it was…or when.' He paused, and since she didn't enlighten him, gathering her composure around her like a protective cloak, he asked evenly, 'Some guy attacked you?'

Rhiannon swallowed. 'Not…exactly.'

CHAPTER SEVEN

NOT exactly? Gabriel wondered what *exactly* she meant by that. A date rape? A petting session that got out of hand, so that she blamed herself for leading the guy on because he didn't stop when she said no? 'If he did something you didn't want him to,' he told her, 'it wasn't your fault.'

Her head came up at that. 'I know it wasn't my fault!'

'Okay,' he said carefully. 'So are you going to tell me what did happen?'

While Rhiannon hesitated, staring at him with wide, unblinking eyes as if hypnotised, heavy footfalls sounded on the tiles below, and then Mick appeared at the foot of the stairs, peering up at them. 'That's coming on, isn't it?' he said. 'Evening, Mr Hudson. Didn't know you were here.'

Gabriel cursed under his breath. 'We're working,' he said curtly, knowing it was no use. The moment had been thoroughly broken.

Mick blinked at Gabriel's tone, and Rhiannon, clearly welcoming the interruption, said, 'We have been, but we've finished now. What do you think?' A smile fixed to her face, she almost ran down the stairs, ranging herself alongside the older man to look upwards but avoiding letting her gaze light on Gabriel.

Gabriel watched her, a peculiar pain squeezing his

chest. She was running from him, relying on another man for protection. From *him*.

Mick looked relieved. 'I'm not much into abstract art,' he confessed. 'But the colours are nice.'

Rhiannon's smile was turned to him. 'I'm glad you like them. You won't get the full effect until it's finished, of course. I'm planning to complete the top half first, so the scaffolding can come down before I do the lower part.'

Tired of being ignored, Gabriel said, 'We're leaving the stuff here overnight, Mick. It should be safe until Rhiannon comes back tomorrow.'

Guessing he wasn't going to get any more out of Rhiannon tonight, Gabriel let Mick escort her out of the building, suppressing a pang of bitterness at the obvious tension leaving her face when he suggested it.

Rhiannon hardly slept. Her mind kept replaying old memories, memories she'd successfully buried now coming back to haunt her.

She knew all the theories about confronting the darkness, bringing her fears into the light of day and reason—she'd been there, done that. And had never intended to go through the process again.

Tonight she'd come too close. And now she was thrown right back to reliving the nightmare, her body possessed by cold, sweating fear, her mind darting frantically about, hunting for escape.

By morning she was consumed with what she knew very well was an unfair resentment against Gabriel.

Determined not to let the demons dictate her actions,

she forced herself to go back to the mosaic. And hoped that Gabriel would have the sensitivity to stay away.

Instead, she found him waiting for her on the stairs.

'I thought,' he said, as she slowly went to meet him, 'we might take up where we left off.'

Rhiannon didn't answer, choking on a range of conflicting emotions—something, she thought with rancour, she was accustomed to in his company—hating him for a variety of reasons, not least of which was the fact that even before she reached the landing she could feel her skin tingling, a liquid heat softening her bones.

Though her gaze resolutely remained on the cans and tools laid out ready, she sensed he was looking at her with that light in his eyes that always made her feel he was trying to penetrate her soul. And she knew he wasn't talking about the mosaic.

Even as part of her jeered at her timidity, she told herself that her past was none of his business, she'd given him no right to delve into it. She cleared her throat of some obstruction, and although her voice wasn't quite normal she made it steady, uncaring. 'I don't need you.'

'Sure? Yesterday we had a pretty good thing going, I thought. Why not carry it through?'

'Yesterday was difficult. I can manage on my own now.'

She set her chin and walked purposefully forward, risking a glance at his face, and seeing it set like a granite mask, only a dismaying glitter in his eyes betraying any emotion.

'Okay.' His voice sounded clipped. 'Whatever you say.'

He didn't stay, taking the stairs up to his office, but later he brought her coffee and one for himself.

Rhiannon reverted to her old habit of resting her back against the stair rail on one side. After one hard, measuring glance, Gabriel took up a matching position at the other side. Stretching his long legs, he looked down into his cup. 'Last night,' he said, 'you started to tell me something.'

'That was a mistake.' Swiftly, she took a gulp of her coffee. 'Anyway, I got over it ages ago.'

'Are you sure?'

'Yes.' She glared at him, the scepticism—almost sarcastic—in his face sending her back to burying her nose again in the cup.

'Did you see a trauma counsellor or someone like that?'

Rhiannon lowered the cup and drew her lips together. 'A psychotherapist,' she admitted reluctantly. 'For nearly a year.'

'Maybe it should have been longer.'

Rhiannon gave an acid little laugh. If he only knew… 'You think I'm loopy?'

'Certainly not. I think you're locking up your emotions and that isn't healthy.'

She tossed off the remainder of the coffee and stood up. Looking down on him, she felt more confident, and the resentment she'd almost lost came flooding back. 'Thanks for your concern. You're not the first man to subject me to this kind of psychoanalysis. All right, I'm sexually repressed and emotionally dysfunctional. Actually I'm perfectly fine with that, thank you.' At least she had been until he came along. And she desperately wanted to return to that circumscribed but secure state of mind—and body. 'If I'm frigid I can live with it.' A loud crackling made her aware that she was crushing the cup in her hand. Distractedly she looked about for a bin.

'Frigid?' Gabriel put down his own cup and stood up, negating her advantage. 'I don't believe that.'

'Believe it. I've been told so by experts—one expert, anyway.' She clamped her mouth shut. She'd talked too much already.

Gabriel looked grimly puzzled. 'Who?'

'Never mind.' Rhiannon dropped the mangled cup onto the drip sheet. She'd dispose of it later. She crossed to the paint and brush she'd been using.

Snake-fast, Gabriel moved and grabbed her arm, bringing her round to face him. 'Your therapist?' he guessed. As if realising the strength of his grip, he dropped his hand, but with her back to the scaffolding and him standing so close she could see herself reflected in his eyes, she couldn't easily escape. 'Was this person any good?' he asked. Patently doubting it.

'He was very well qualified, and he has a respected reputation.' Something he hadn't hesitated to remind her of.

Frowning, Gabriel said, 'Did you ever ask for a second opinion?'

She gave another brittle laugh. 'I've had plenty of second opinions. Yours is only the latest.'

His mouth tightened again. 'It wasn't some crude line to coerce you into sex. I wanted to help.'

He was close enough for her to lean on his chest if she wanted to…and she did want to. Instead she braced herself. 'I don't need help. Not yours, not anyone's.'

'All right,' he said after a moment, his gaze unblinking. 'If you say so.'

He didn't believe her. Nettled, she turned away from him again and stalked back to the wall.

'You've hardly had five minutes' break,' Gabriel pointed out, sounding unusually irritable.

'I just want to get on with it.'

Gabriel tossed the remainder of his coffee down his throat, and muttered almost inaudibly, 'So do I.'

He stuck around, watching in a rather brooding fashion, giving her a distinct feeling that he was purposely trying to unsettle her with his silent, watchful presence. She worked more slowly than usual, afraid of making some mistake because she couldn't shake her prickly awareness of him, yet determined not to let him know it.

After what seemed an age, he left, and she didn't see him again before Mick let her out of the building.

The next time he stopped by to check progress his casually helpful manner had returned, and he said nothing, did nothing that Mick might not have done.

He didn't bring up the subject of her past again, and Rhiannon told herself that he'd forgotten all about her near-confession. She thrust the episode to the back of her mind, and gradually relaxed her vigilance, sometimes scarcely noticing Gabriel's visits, except for the tingling warmth that told her he was near.

She finished mortaring the top half on a Sunday afternoon while Gabriel watched. She pressed the last tessera into place and stood up. 'I can't go any further here until the mortar cures.'

Gabriel offered her a hand as she climbed down to the landing, and without even thinking about it, she let him help her. Putting her other hand to her back, with a rueful grimace she said, 'I need some exercise.'

'How about a walk down to the waterfront?' Gabriel suggested. 'We could have a drink. This deserves a celebration.'

'Dressed like this?' Realising he still held her hand, she tugged it away and plucked at the front of the stained shirt she wore.

'It doesn't matter,' he said, 'but I can lend you a clean shirt if you like.'

Remembering what had happened last time they were together in his office, Rhiannon felt a knot tighten in her stomach, but he gave no sign of sharing her discomfort. Lately he'd seemed to be taking pains to put her at ease, with no probing into her private life. She knew by now that he would back off at the least hint that she was feeling crowded or threatened.

Beginning to shake her head, she paused. 'You keep spare clothes here?'

'Uh-huh. Sometimes it's more convenient than going home to change.'

She too sometimes changed before leaving work, keeping jeans and a couple of T-shirts and tank tops there for the purpose.

Her gaze fixed firmly on his face, she said, 'All right.'

Gabriel stopped himself from grabbing her and planting a kiss on her lips there and then. Instead he acted casual, leading the way up to his office and pulling a white evening shirt from a dry-cleaner's bag. 'There's a wash-room through there,' he said, indicating a door.

When she emerged, with the sleeves of the shirt rolled to her elbows and the tails tied about her waist, her own garment in her hand, he allowed himself only one swift, comprehensive glance, though he couldn't resist commenting, 'Looks better on you.' And to keep his hands from reaching for her and tearing the garment right off again, he turned abruptly to the door. 'Let's go.' She'd be safer in the street, where the presence of other people would inhibit his baser instincts. He had worked too hard at gaining her confidence to spoil it now.

They strolled past the graffiti-covered boards that hid the site next door, where the spoil had been carted away and diggers had begun on the foundations for a new building, and on down Queen Street to the Viaduct Basin. Among the numerous bars and restaurants Gabriel found one with outdoor seating where they could watch the water lapping against the wharves and admire the anchored yachts.

Gabriel ordered a bottle of sparkling wine. 'Something to eat?' he asked Rhiannon.

'If we're going to drink a bottle…' she said.

He grinned, and handed her the menu. 'How about a plate of nachos to share?'

They settled for that, and picked companionably at the generous dish while having a desultory conversation, until Rhiannon yawned and said, 'Excuse me.'

'I'm that boring?' Gabriel inquired.

She laughed, shaking her head. 'You know it isn't that. You're the least boring man I know.'

He actually felt his heart skip a beat. 'How many men do you know?' he asked lightly.

She was dipping a crisp nacho triangle into sour cream. Her eyes lowered, she went on jabbing the corner into the soft mass. 'A few.'

He wondered how well. At a guess, not very. But there was Peri...

She put the nacho into her mouth, half turning to watch the ferry tie up, the ramp rattle down for the passengers. 'When I was a kid my parents used to take me on weekends to the North Shore for the day.'

'We could do that,' he offered.

She looked at him with surprise, then a smile curved her mouth. 'Really?'

Curbing a devout sense of astonished thankfulness, Gabriel shrugged. 'Why not?'

They took the next boat out, making their way to the bow where the sea breeze tugged at Rhiannon's hair and whipped colour into her cheeks. The city receded as the boat headed across choppy little white-tipped waves, strewn with small craft, multicoloured sails dipping and swaying, and motor launches cutting foam paths in the water. Distantly the islands of the Hauraki Gulf rose gently from the sea.

'Do you want to sit down?' Gabriel asked.

Rhiannon shook her head. A strand of hair blew over her eyes and she brushed it aside. He wondered if she knew how it moulded the fabric of her shirt to her breasts. He wrenched his eyes away. Something in the water caught his gaze, and he automatically put an arm about Rhiannon's shoulder, pointing. 'Look over there.'

A dolphin arched, glistening, from the waves, then

another joined it. Rhiannon gasped, and he looked down to see wonder on her face. Other people were exclaiming, and the speaker system blared into life, advising passengers of dolphins on the right.

The animals played about for some minutes, then disappeared, and the excitement on board died down.

Rhiannon shivered and wrapped her arms about herself.

'Are you cold?' Gabriel inquired. 'We could go inside.'

'No, it's more fun out here.' But she shivered again, and without thinking he altered his position, moving behind her and wrapping both arms about her waist.

He felt her slight stiffening, and clenched his jaw, prepared to release her. Then to his considerable astonishment she relaxed, her shoulder resting on his chest, her back warming his, her sweet behind tantalisingly nestled against…

Don't go there.

He closed his eyes, but the pictures his imagination conjured didn't help. Opening his eyes again, he kept them wide until the wind stung them, hoping the pain would coerce his rebellious body into submission. A spatter of spray over the bow sent a few cold droplets into his face, as Rhiannon laughed and ducked her head.

It would take more than that to kill the heat that was burning him up, but he grabbed the chance to loosen his hold just a little, easing his lower body away. When the boat finally reached the shore he was torn between relief and reluctance as she moved and went ahead of him to disembark.

*   *   *

Rhiannon couldn't remember when she'd last done anything so spontaneous. Maybe the couple of glasses of bubbly she'd drunk had something to do with it.

But it was also the man who was sharing this mini-adventure. With Gabriel at her side there was no need to guard against unwelcome attention, to shy away from an admiring glance or a cheeky grin, or experience an uncomfortable prickle of warning down her spine when, strolling along a path above the water, they had to skirt a lounging lone male on a park seat, whose legs almost blocked the narrow path.

Gabriel walked with his hands in his pockets, then at a lower point jumped down onto the sandy beach and turned to take her hand while she did the same.

Rhiannon slipped off her sneakers and allowed the waves to wash over her feet as she had when she was a child. Gabriel stood by, a slight grin on his face.

She bent to pick a scallop shell out of the sand, pink, frilled and perfect, and went to join him, showing him her find before walking along the beach at his side.

She felt light, untrammelled—and happy.

The realisation was like a starburst of light around her. She momentarily lost her footing in the soft sand and stumbled, bumping Gabriel's arm as he steadied her with a tight grip on her hand.

Nearby a group of children chased one another in and out of the shallows, squealing. Somewhere a dog was barking. A couple walked by, arms about each other, a transistor radio blaring in the man's hand.

Rhiannon was oblivious to it all, lost in the smile that Gabriel slanted down at her.

'You okay?' he asked, a line appearing between his brows.

I'm in love, she thought, stunned. *This is how it feels to be in love.*

'Yes,' she said, unable to tear her gaze from him. 'Yes, I'm okay.'

Dimly she remembered similar sensations from her early teens, though nothing like this. Nothing so utterly certain, so deeply felt, so unwavering, and so…shattering.

'Rhiannon?' He lifted his free hand, touching her cheek with his fingers. 'What is it?'

She swallowed hard, and gave him a shaky smile back. 'I turned my ankle a bit.'

Immediately the frown deepened. He went down on one knee, saying, 'Show me! This one?' Strong fingers encircled her right ankle, giving her a small shock of something she couldn't put a name to as he looked up at her interrogatively.

'Gabriel!' She tried a shaky laugh. 'It's all right now, really.'

'You're sure?' When she nodded, he straightened and took possession of her hand again. 'You would tell me if you're hurt?'

'It was nothing. Truly.'

'Promise you won't lie to me.' He looked grave and intent.

'I won't.' Euphoria mingled with sick dismay and then panic.

Everything in her world had changed in a moment. She didn't have a clue what to do about it. 'I'm fine,' she said, already breaking her promise. What would he say if she told him she'd just discovered she loved him? She began walking again, forcing him to follow.

They climbed to the grass verge opposite the shopping centre, and Gabriel smiled as she tried to wipe sand from her feet, sitting on a set of steps leading from the beach to the shopping area. 'Use this,' he offered, pulling out a pristine handkerchief.

'It's too clean!'

'It'll wash. Take it.'

'Well…thanks.' She took it and did the best she could, then picked up a shoe and put it on.

Gabriel had the other in his hand. Kneeling a couple of steps below her, he grasped her ankle and slipped the shoe onto her foot. When he stood and offered her his hand, she was slightly dizzy.

They investigated a few open shops, and lost themselves for a while in a rabbit warren masquerading as a secondhand book store, emerging with a small bundle of books each.

Gabriel said, 'What say we eat here before we go back to the city?'

The sun was setting as they ordered their dinner and then opened their book parcels to inspect each other's choices. By the time they'd finished their meal and boarded the return ferry it was dark.

A girl in high-heeled boots, similar to those Peri had persuaded Rhiannon into, tripped somehow at the end of the ramp, landing on her knees, and Gabriel stepped forward to help her up.

The girl pushed a mane of curly red hair from her eyes, which widened as they lit on her rescuer. 'Thank you,' she said breathlessly, leaning on his arm.

'Okay.' He steadied her and dropped his hands, returning to Rhiannon's side.

Watching the girl's mouth droop in disappointment, Rhiannon couldn't help a sympathetic little laugh.

'Funny?' Gabriel asked, guiding her to a seat.

'Of course not. She isn't hurt, is she?'

'Nope. Those boots can be lethal, though. In more ways than one.' He cast her a sideways grin. 'How are yours?'

'I haven't worn them again. They were Peri's idea.'

'Peri's?'

'He said I couldn't go out wi—to something like that wearing my work clothes, and he took me shopping.'

'*Took* you?'

'He chose everything I wore that night.'

Gabriel was staring at her. 'Peri? He's *gay?*'

'A man doesn't have to be gay to be interested in clothes, but actually, yes. Does that shock you?'

'No! No,' he said. 'I should have guessed.'

In the distance they could see the approaching lights of the buildings and roadways edging the harbour. Rhiannon yawned and Gabriel pulled her close under his arm, elated when she laid her head against his chest and let her eyelids drift down.

She trusted him enough to fall asleep in his arms. It was a huge, gigantic step but he was aware he mustn't mess up now. He'd have to tread carefully to build on the undoubted gains he'd made.

When the ferry docked she woke, but seemed almost to be in a dream until they reached the street and Gabriel hailed a taxi. Then she turned to him, the dazed look in her eyes beginning to dissipate. 'We're not walking back to the building?'

'I'm taking you home. You're not fit to drive.'

'My car...' she protested as he bundled her into the rear seat and climbed in after her, giving the driver the address.

'I'll get Mick to keep an eye on it.' He took out his mobile phone and started punching numbers into it, left a terse message and put the phone back in his pocket.

'I have had more wine than I'm used to,' Rhiannon admitted, stifling another yawn. They'd finished off a bottle at dinner.

'And you've been working all hours on that damned mosaic.'

She laughed. 'It's your mosaic. I thought you liked it.'

'You're exhausted.'

'I'm *tired,*' she corrected. 'And it isn't your fault.'

He hadn't claimed it was, but she'd put her finger on the cause of his irritation.

'I should have sent you home to rest,' he muttered, 'instead of taking you off on a mad day trip.'

'I didn't need rest. And I've had a wonderful day.'

She reached out and touched his hand for a fraction of a second, and the effect on him was electric. Rhiannon wasn't given to spontaneous touching, and didn't even appear to realise she'd done it. He had to take several breaths before he could trust himself to say anything. 'I'm glad,' he managed.

Hardly a riveting speech. Fortunately she didn't seem to expect one; just gave him a sleepy smile and turned to stare out of the cab window, the passing streetlights giving him flickering glimpses of her profile and the slight, smiling curve on her mouth.

When they arrived he told the cabbie to wait and went with her to the door. 'If you give me your key,' he said, 'I'll see your car is taken to the parking building.'

She took the key off the ring she'd pulled from the pocket of her jeans, and put it in his outstretched hand. Looking away from him to the waiting taxi, she said hesitantly, 'If you'd like to come in…'

Gabriel held his breath. What did she have in mind? Whatever it was, he didn't trust himself not to take advantage of her uncharacteristic invitation once they were inside. And that wouldn't be fair. For one thing, he couldn't be sure it wasn't the wine talking. For another, she was dead tired and needed to sleep. 'I'll take a rain-check on that,' he said.

Wondering if he was being a total fool, he bent and kissed her cheek, then left before he could be tempted to change his mind.

'You must be in love,' Peri said.

'What?' Startled, Rhiannon looked up, the book she'd been going to shelve forgotten in her hands.

'You've been standing there for the last five minutes staring at nothing. And you haven't heard a word I've said to you.'

Flushing, she said, 'I'm sorry, Peri. I was thinking.'

'It's your angel Gabriel, isn't it? And I don't mean the mosaic. How's it going, by the way?'

'I'll be grouting the top next week.'

Which meant she'd be halfway. More, really, because the bottom half would be easier. She had mixed feelings about the looming completion of the project, eager to get to the end and see her vision come to fruition, yet knowing it would signal a change in her relationship with Gabriel.

For weeks, the sexual hunger emanating from him that both confused and excited her had become muted to the point of non-existence. Sometimes she'd wondered if he'd given up on her after all, deciding not to waste time on a woman who couldn't give him what he wanted.

That ought to have set her mind at rest, not engendered a strange hollow ache in her chest.

The realisation that she had fallen in love with him brought excruciating new complications and dilemmas. It was both exhilarating and frightening.

When Rhiannon started filling in the spaces between the tesserae with grouting, Gabriel offered his long arms for the top corner. She kept a critical eye on him, and when she took over gave him the task of sponging off the excess grouting before it dried.

After working for some time she stripped off her gloves and wiped her forehead, then flexed her stiffening right arm.

'Enough for now,' Gabriel said. 'You're stronger than you look, but this is hard yakker for you, and I'm hungry. Did you eat before you came here?'

'I had a salad.'

'Salad!' He sounded disgusted. 'You need something more substantial than that. Why don't we go somewhere for a proper meal?'

Rhiannon indicated her shirt and jeans, streaked with patches of grouting. Even her rubber-soled canvas shoes hadn't escaped. The loan of a shirt wouldn't help much this time. 'You're joking.'

'Take-aways then,' Gabriel decided. 'What would you like? Chinese? Indian? Fish, sausages, oysters?'

The idea had its appeal, now that he mentioned it. 'Chinese,' Rhiannon said.

While she packed up her materials he went off to get it, returning with a large bag from which delicious smells wafted, a folded newspaper tucked under his arm. 'We can take this up to my office,' he suggested. 'More comfortable than sitting on the stairs.'

Leading the way, he tossed the newspaper on the coffee table and put down the paper bag. When she emerged from the washroom after tidying and washing as well as she could, he had opened a cupboard and brought out plates, forks and wineglasses, then like a conjurer produced a bottle of wine.

It was a feast, and the fruity wine added to it.

After they'd finished eating, Rhiannon sat back in the corner of the sofa, still with a half-full glass in her hand. Gabriel, on the same sofa but a couple of feet away, was pouring more wine into his glass.

He proffered the bottle, but she shook her head. 'If you want your mosaic done right, don't ply me with wine.'

'You're not going to do any more tonight?'

'I'd like to finish that upper half,' Rhiannon said, 'and then you could get rid of the scaffolding.' She looked at her watch.

'All right, no more wine. How do you feel about apples?'

'Apples?' Rhiannon repeated blankly. There were none on the table.

'It's biblical,' Gabriel said. 'Never mind.'

He leaned back into the other corner of the sofa, one arm along its back, his eyes lazily on her.

Rhiannon finished her wine, and bent forward to put her glass on the table. The newspaper, folded in half, caught her eye, showing part of a photograph. A handsome, trim middle-aged man had his back to the camera as he walked away, but his face was half turned, an outstretched hand apparently motioning the photographer away.

Rhiannon leaned a little closer, her heart pounding, her temples, too. It couldn't be…

It was. She knew the face, though it was years since she'd seen the man.

On autopilot, her hand stretched out even as her mind recoiled. She clutched at the paper and the fold straightened in her hand, showing the headline above the picture.

Therapist Accused it said in bold type.

Her gaze dropped to the first paragraph of the story.

Psychotherapist Gerald Dodd, accused by two former clients of sexual misconduct while they were being treated by him, refused to talk with our reporter after his appearance in court on Friday…

The words swirled before her eyes. Her hands started shaking, rattling the paper, and she dropped it onto her knees.

Gerald Dodd. The name echoed in her mind. She looked down again at the photograph, trying to take it in.

'Rhiannon?' Gabriel's voice was urgent. 'What's the matter?'

She looked up with dazed eyes, scarcely seeing him. In her mind she was sitting in a stuffy, badly lit room where a persistent fly buzzed against the Venetian blind vainly trying to find freedom. While Gerald Dodd, a hand on her knee, gazed into her eyes with a compassionate brown stare and said, 'The condition of frigidity is curable, you know. I can help you.'

'*Rhiannon?*' The eyes looking into hers, coming closer and then halting as Gabriel checked his movement towards her, were silver-grey. 'Are you sick?'

She probably looked sick. Her head was swimming, and she felt cold all over. There was sweat on her forehead.

'I know him,' she whispered.

Gabriel shifted his gaze to the newspaper in her lap and reached for it, his eyes darkening. 'Someone died?'

He frowned down at the headlines, then his head jerked up. 'You know this man?'

Unable to speak, still less to prevaricate, Rhiannon nodded.

Gabriel dropped his head, skimming the words, opening out the remaining fold to see the rest of the story.

He looked up, his face drawn almost as though he were in pain. 'He was your therapist?' he queried. 'The one who said you were frigid?'

Again she nodded, still frozen in shock.

His lips formed a silent swearword. Harshly he asked, 'Did he do this to you, too?'

The pages he held blurred before her eyes. 'I... h-haven't read it all,' she said.

'Sexual assault,' Gabriel said bluntly, distaste in his voice, his expression. He tossed the paper aside. 'The bastard took advantage of his patients, offered them what he called sexual therapy. He says they consented.'

'He would,' she said. 'He'd have listened to them pour out their most intimate secrets for months, given them sympathy, support, got closer to them in some ways than their own mothers. Made them dependent on him. Promised to cure them, help them to a normal state of mind and a happy life if they'd just trust him. That's how he…operated.'

But she'd known that it wasn't right. Confused and vulnerable though she'd been, at least she'd retained enough common sense to reject the specious arguments Gerald Dodd had put forward, recognising them for what they were.

Gabriel's eyes had darkened, and his face might have been carved in stone. 'Did you report him?'

Rhiannon shook her head. 'No one would have believed me. He told me that. He was a highly respected professional, and I was…a disturbed young woman.'

Gabriel seemed for a moment to have lost his usual composure. He looked so angry she drew a quick breath, and her hands fluttered in her lap.

He held out his own hands to her, his eyes softening, although his mouth hadn't lost its grim look.

Almost without thought, she reached out to him, and the warmth of his fingers flowed into hers and up her arms, until her whole body began to lose its sudden chill.

'He said…he said patients often deluded themselves about their therapist, imagined things that had never happened. I knew I hadn't imagined anything, but he nearly convinced me. I could see he'd have no problem convincing any inquiry.'

'Bastard!' Gabriel muttered. He ran his hands up her arms, holding her shoulders gently.

Rhiannon was trembling, feeling like a doe running from the hounds, having blundered into some kind of sanctuary.

She couldn't look up. Fixing her gaze on Gabriel's chin, she saw the tightening of the muscles along his jawline.

He moved his hands from her shoulders, gliding them along her back, drawing her closer until she rested against him. His hold on her was very light, and his cheek just touched her temple. 'The man's a criminal,' he said. 'A predator of the worst kind, picking the most defenceless victims. I hope he rots in jail for years.'

'Thank you,' Rhiannon whispered.

'For what?' He eased away and looked down at her.

'For believing me,' she said. 'For being so angry on my behalf. For…comforting me. Though not with apples.' She tried to smile, lifting her head to look back at him.

Gabriel didn't smile, but the angry light in his eyes faded. 'So you do know the quotation,' he said.

It was filtering through from some recess of her mind, words spoken at a long-ago occasion—perhaps a friend's wedding. '"Stay me with flagons,"' she quoted, '"and comfort me with apples."'

'From the *Song of Songs*,' Gabriel said, and even as she recalled the next lines he recited them, his voice slow and deep. '"…for I am sick with love."'

Watching her eyelids flutter down on the deepened colour in her cheeks, he smiled. 'Rhiannon?'

He saw the effort it took for her to look up and meet his eyes. 'Yes?' she said on a breath.

Her lips, tempting and full, and a little unsteady, were inches from him, and she didn't move, didn't turn her head or pull away, her body soft and pliant against his, although there was a hint of nervousness in her eyes.

'Rhiannon?' he said again, his voice scarcely a murmur. He could feel her heart beating against his chest, under the tempting mound of her breasts.

'Yes,' she said again, answering the question in his eyes.

Momentarily he closed his own eyes and offered up a silent prayer of thankfulness. Then he narrowed the gap between their mouths and felt her tremble, felt the sweet, unsure welcome of her lips as he parted them with his kiss.

CHAPTER EIGHT

RHIANNON floated on a sea of sensation. Gabriel was seducing her with his mouth, offering much more than comfort and compassion. His lips on hers were careful yet questing, asking, not demanding, not aggressive. Coaxing her mouth to open for him. Showing her what a kiss could be.

At first merely quiescent, afraid to do anything for fear of spoiling the fragile flowering of the most exquisite feelings she'd ever known, within moments she dared to kiss him back, a tentative, perhaps clumsy answering pressure of her lips mimicking his. Shyly she draped her arms about his neck, creating a tiny friction of her peaking breasts against his chest. She slid a hand inside his shirt, her fingers fumbling open the button that frustrated her further exploration.

His whole body froze into stillness; she felt it. Her heart plunging, she drew back as far as his hand behind her head would allow. 'Sorry,' she said stumblingly, confused. 'Did I do something wrong?'

Gabriel made an odd, strangled sound. 'No, sweetheart! You did something very right.' Then he lowered his mouth again to hers and she drowned in desire.

Dimly she knew that was what it was—the lovely warmth in her veins turning to a melting heat as Gabriel delicately, deliciously, encouraged her deeper into the kiss, her mouth opening further under his while his arm braced her bowed body, his chest hard against her aching, tingling breasts.

His hand slid to her nape, then under her raised arm until it found her madly beating heart, and tenderly cupped her breast.

'Oh!' Rhiannon exclaimed into his mouth. A hot shiver started under his hand and passed right over her body, weakening her limbs.

Gabriel lifted his head, his hand abandoning her breast, both arms encircling her. 'If I'm going too fast for you,' he said, and rested his forehead on hers, 'it's all right. We'll take it at your pace, Rhiannon.'

Her heart seemed to turn into a molten pool. He'd misunderstood, but his immediate reaction surprised and touched her.

She raised her face to his, skimmed his mouth with hers, and his arms tightened again, his mouth tender and persuasive as her lips trembled open for him.

Everything dissolved into a haze around her, the only thing that mattered any more was this astonishing, mindless wanting, centred on Gabriel, and how he made her feel, drowning in sensation. He pressed her into the cushions behind her, muttering, 'It's the wrong place and the wrong time, but what the hell…'

Before she had time to think he was kissing her again, and all thought flew away, replaced by ever more stunning waves of pleasure.

She felt strangely outside herself, her mind a separate entity from the body in Gabriel's arms, hands clutching his shoulders, and pulling open buttons so she could feel his skin against hers. Was this really her?

His fingers too opened buttons and zips and she shuddered when his hands found her warm flesh, making him draw back again. 'No?' he queried, his eyes ablaze, his cheeks darkened with colour.

'Yes,' Rhiannon said on a choking laugh, and drew his head back to her. 'Don't stop.'

He shuddered then, too, and gave a deep guttural sound of satisfaction, his mouth drawing a path from the hurrying pulse at her throat down to the throbbing centre of a breast.

Her teeth bit into her lower lip to stop a cry of shocked delight, and she thrust her hands into his hair, loving the surprising, silky softness of it. She seemed to be soaring into another level of existence, every touch, every increasingly intimate kiss bringing her closer to some kind of pinnacle that was just out of reach.

Then Gabriel stopped kissing her, sliding them both to the carpeted floor, arranging cushions under her, taking off her jeans, kissing her navel, her thighs, touching her in ways she'd never dreamed of.

'We should have a bed,' he groaned. She realised he was wearing only his jeans, his shirt discarded. His chest gleamed with a faint film of sweat. But it was beautiful. She reached out a hand to touch him, and he closed his eyes, his face going taut as he balanced himself above her. His big palm covered her hand, and he held it over the drumbeat of his heart.

He opened his eyes and they were pure silver, sheened with desire. 'You're sure you don't want to stop?' he said, his voice gritty and barely audible. 'Because from now on it's going to be damned difficult.'

Wordlessly, Rhiannon shook her head. She was scared, but elated, too. Dazed with a new kind of excitement, caught in a tide wash of new experiences, a lightning storm of sensation.

Gabriel stroked her hair back from her hot face, kissed her quickly and said, 'Just a second.'

He evaded her clinging hands and she closed her eyes, suddenly cold as he moved away from her and she heard the opening and closing of a drawer.

Instinctively she covered her bared breasts with her hands, and faint alarm momentarily chilled her. What was she doing? Did she *know* what she was doing?

Then she felt Gabriel's arms around her, folding her close to his warm strong body, and realised he was naked.

She clutched at him, at the warmth and strength of him that would dispel her fear, and when he kissed her again she melted into him, kissed him back feverishly, felt him surge against her and welcomed him with a mixture of relief, triumph and nervous tension.

He stroked her, whispered kisses against her skin, caressed her into a mindless, burning desire before he nudged at the entrance of her womanhood, and her legs of their own accord parted to cradle him.

He entered slowly, gently, and stilled when he found a slight resistance. Muttering something she didn't catch, he began to withdraw, but she dug her fingers into his shoulders and said, her voice muffled against his shoulder, 'No! Please…go on.'

He kissed her then, blindingly, forgetting gentleness for a moment, and there was a searing pain at his possession, her automatic protest quelled under his mouth.

Gabriel lifted his head and she saw anguish in his face. 'Rhiannon…' he said hoarsely.

'It's all right,' she whispered, lifting clumsily to meet him.

He groaned, and moved, too, cautiously, his jaw set as he watched her face. 'Are you all right?' he grated.

'Yes!' She looked back at him fiercely, and he groaned again, kissed her equally fiercely, moved until she matched his rhythm, and her eyes fluttered closed, her lips parting as at last he took her to the elusive pinnacle and flung her over the edge into a vortex of exquisite sensation.

He was not far behind, his lips against her neck as his climax gripped him and he convulsed deliciously in his release.

Rhiannon's hands slipped from Gabriel's shoulders, and he loosened his hold, taking his weight from her. 'One thing we know,' he said, a crooked grin belying the heated glitter that remained in his eyes, 'you're not frigid.'

Not with him, obviously. The knowledge should be liberating, and certainly one part of her rejoiced but another was dismayed.

How quickly comfort had turned to passion. A passion that in retrospect was frightening in its depth and intensity.

Gabriel had the power to make her lose control—of herself, her body, her emotions. That was a revelation—and a shock. There had been no planning, unless the fact that he'd been prepared indicated a plan. No measured weighing of the wisdom of what they were doing, not even a bed. Only a sudden, impromptu coupling on the floor.

Gabriel watched the emotions flit across her face. She hadn't yet regained her composure, and her conflicted feelings were naked to him. As her body had been.

Slamming the door on that thought, he concentrated on interpreting her expressions. He saw when she deliberately closed down, shut him out, and inwardly he cursed.

Rhiannon eased away from him, reaching for her clothes.

'Don't,' he said urgently, fighting his need to hold her, pull her back into his arms. 'Don't run away from me again.'

Rhiannon's chin came up. 'I'm not running anywhere.'

Not physically, but in her mind she was retreating— he could almost see the doors being locked against him, one after another, making her inaccessible.

He wouldn't allow it. Couldn't. 'Rhiannon,' he said, 'we can't pretend this didn't happen.'

Buttoning her shirt, she turned her head aside, the habit exasperating him so much that he shot out a hand and grasped her chin, forcing her to look at him again. 'That might be how you've dealt with your problems in the past,' he said, 'but it won't wash this time.' Not that he understood exactly why making love together should be a problem, given her recent responses, but he could see she still had one. He felt her jaw tense under the tender skin against his fingers and, realising what he was doing, he dropped his hand. *'Talk to me.'*

Instead she stubbornly went on dressing as if her life depended on it.

Reluctantly he pulled on his jeans, ready to face her

when she got up. He stood before her, blocking the way the door.

Her eyes were jewel-bright. She took a step back from him, and as always that stabbed his heart. 'It was a mistake,' she said. 'You have no idea how I've dealt with my problems! How I've managed to make some kind of normal existence for myself.'

In a split second Gabriel made a decision. He had a choice—to placate her, apologise and let her crawl back into her protective shell—or take advantage of her rare loss of control and goad her into revealing more of her carefully guarded secrets.

He took the riskier path. 'An existence?' he repeated derisively. 'That's not a life!'

'It's my life! It's what I want.'

'You want *me!*' he flung at her. 'Just now, you wanted me! And you had me.' He couldn't stop the ring of triumph from colouring his voice. It had been such a buzz, such an overwhelming relief when her lips moved under his, inexpert but eager, when she'd followed instinct and bowed her body to his, when he'd felt the hardened centres of her breast and his hand had found the rounded fullness with its tantalising bud. And once she'd indicated her willingness to follow through, he hadn't had the power to resist his instincts.

She went pale, and a tug of compunction pierced him. 'Why deny it?' he asked, anguish gentling his tone. 'Why let whatever happened in the past stop you from having a future?'

'I'm not! I haven't.'

'That's what it looks like to me.' He was relentless, not daring to backtrack now. 'So maybe you've come a long way—' he could only guess how far and at what cost '—but not far enough.'

'What would you know?' she demanded.

'*Damn all!*' His own raised voice shocked him. 'Because you won't *tell* me anything!' He hadn't realised that he too was furious. Furious and frustrated.

Rhiannon blinked, her face going taut, but she didn't physically recoil. He took some kind of odd pleasure in that. She wasn't afraid of him, perhaps bolstered by her own rage. 'I did tell you,' she said, 'about Dr Dodd.'

'Because you were in shock and couldn't bottle it up anymore. Why were you seeing him in the first place?'

He saw instantly that the approach was too blunt. Her eyes went blank, wariness freezing her expression. Something tightened his own facial muscles, making it difficult for him to breathe. How bad could it have been to make her look like that, even her lips going white, as if she was too numbed to say anything?

Realising he couldn't press that point, Gabriel returned to the previous one. 'And what are you going to do about him?'

'Do?' She blinked again. Her voice was faint but at least she wasn't speechless anymore, and a slight colour tempered the alarming pallor of her cheeks and lips. 'What do you mean?'

'You did nothing before, and now he has more victims.'

Her eyes widened. 'That's not my fault!'

'No.' He allowed her that. 'But other women have come forward and he'll be held accountable at last. You have the chance to make your complaint now and be heard.'

'In court?' Her whole body seemed to shrink. 'They have two witnesses. There's no need.'

'For your own sake.'

'I don't need revenge.'

She sounded sure of herself, but he was still sceptical. Perhaps she saw it in his face. 'And I don't need your advice,' she said, her expression completely shuttered.

End of conversation. Unbelievably, she went to the table and began packing up empty containers, unsteady fingers shoving them into the bag. He wanted to shake her, yell at her to open herself up to him, show him what lurked in the shadows of her mind so that he could help her.

Which would be guaranteed to send her further back into the depths she claimed to have climbed from.

Gabriel thrust his hair from his forehead and went to pick up the wine, pouring the last of it into his glass and tossing it down his throat. He could see she was trying in some pathetic way to blot that blinding lovemaking from her mind. Exasperated pity squeezed his heart even while he burned with angry disappointment. 'Leave those,' he advised roughly as Rhiannon stacked the plates. 'My secretary will take care of them.'

She straightened. 'Thank you.' She wasn't looking at him, but after a pause she lifted her eyes to his, though he could see it wasn't easy.

He knew better than to kiss her stubborn, vulnerable mouth. 'You're welcome,' he said, his voice laden with deliberate irony. 'Any time.'

'I'll get back to work,' she said thinly. 'I can do that last bit on my own.'

Back to work? Gabriel blinked, then stifled a bitter

laugh. This was part of her determination to wipe out what had happened between them, as if it were some unimportant interruption that could be put aside by absorbing herself in her art.

Two could play at that. Succumbing to black anger, before she reached the door he said as remotely as he could manage, 'Let me know if you need anything. I'll be working here.' To add to the effect he went to the desk and randomly shuffled some papers.

Fleetingly she looked back. 'Thanks. I'm very grateful.'

Yeah, Gabriel thought sourly when the door had closed behind her. Grateful that he wasn't going to keep her company, distracting her from her concentration on cold, hard tiles—albeit broken ones. On his spiritual namesake who was above earthly-and earthy—things like sex and desire.

His shirt lay crumpled and forgotten on the floor, rather spoiling his attempt to emulate Rhiannon's return to normality.

He picked it up and buttoned himself into it, impatiently shoving the ends into his pants, wondering if Rhiannon even remembered the eagerness with which she'd helped him out of it. Her fingers had been unsteady and unsure, but when they touched his naked skin he'd had to clench his teeth to keep some self-control, afraid he was about to jump the gun like some horny teenager.

Tossing aside the papers he'd just muddled up, he sank heavily into the chair behind his desk, thrusting his fingers through his hair. Rhiannon had done that, too, in the heat of passion, making his neck—his whole body—tingle with pleasure.

Abruptly he sat straighter, reaching for the on-button on his computer, bringing up a column of figures. He'd said he was going to work. If she could, so could he. He'd always had the ability to switch his concentration to his job and keep it there, no matter what. No woman had ever stopped him before.

But how shyly Rhiannon had slid her hands about his neck, her back arching against his arm. And her mouth…

Oh God, her mouth. And her lovely breasts with their pink, budded centres, her skin like smooth silk, and then the snug, satiny depths that had welcomed him, even though…

Even though…

It hit him with a blinding force. That unexpected, brief difficulty, when he'd been afraid he was hurting her, had been more than just an indication of a long abstinence. It was something else. Something new in his experience.

He stared at the screen until the numbers danced before him and his eyes stung.

She'd been a *virgin*.

A sudden chill passed over him. He broke into a cold sweat.

Surely she had admitted that Gerald Dodd had assaulted her? Rapidly reviewing what she'd actually said, Gabriel swore quietly.

He'd made assumptions—wrong assumptions.

Whatever Dodd had done to Rhiannon had undoubtedly been unethical and evil, but…

But, a thin, relentless inner voice accused, growing stronger and louder until it thundered in his ears, hadn't Gabriel himself just done something similar? Maybe-the thought hit him like a blow to his stomach—even worse?

Instead of listening properly, finding out what had really happened, reassuring her with words, he'd taken advantage of the moment. Sure, he'd obtained her tacit consent before he kissed her, and he'd meant it to be a chaste kiss, almost brotherly…well, perhaps not quite that, but a kiss of comfort, rather than passion. Nothing to make her anxious or afraid.

Then she'd kissed him back, and all his pious, specious reasoning went out the window along with his self-control.

At least he'd retained enough decency to keep a rein on his desire and not scare her to death. And to pause, difficult though it had been, when she made that little sound, like a whimper of distress.

Or pleasure…

He hadn't been sure. But when he'd held back to determine the cause she'd begged him to go on.

And he'd realised how much further he'd penetrated into her defences than he had meant or expected to.

Only, he reminded himself brutally, because they'd already been weakened by that blasted news report.

Why hadn't he stopped himself there? She'd still been in shock, as he'd said himself, and he'd had no right to use it to further his own rampant desire for her. Which brought him full circle.

Bile rose in his throat—revulsion at the thought of having anything in common with Gerald Dodd.

It's not the same! he told himself. Of course it wasn't.

Because…? the merciless inner voice jeered.

Because it wasn't just sex he wanted from Rhiannon. Because it hadn't been enough. Never would be.

He wanted her smile, her talent, her enthusiasm for

her work, her understanding of what art was, her rare laughter, her intensity, and the warmth that she showed Peri and Mick Dysart, sometimes even her customers—but not nearly often enough to himself.

He wanted to free her from the constraints that prevented her showing him that side of her personality. From whatever horrors in her past were haunting her.

He didn't only want to make love to her—he wanted to chase the shadows from her eyes, protect her from louts like the one they'd encountered in the café, and from sleazy sexual opportunists like Gerald Dodd. Even—he groaned, and dropped his head into his hands—from himself.

He wanted to make her happy. Ever after.

No excuse, he reminded himself sternly, absorbing the stunning knowledge that he wanted Rhiannon in his life forever. It didn't make what he had done to her any less selfish.

Or help him devise a strategy to make up for it.

Half an hour later he let her out of the building, and she said, 'You could have the scaffolding taken down now. If there's any touching up to do on that part I can use a stepladder. There's no need to block the stairway any longer.'

'I'll get rid of it,' he promised.

'Thanks for your help,' she said hurriedly, as he opened the door. 'My car's just over there. I'll be all right now.'

He caught her arm. 'Rhiannon—I'm sorry. I took advantage and I should have had more sense—and more willpower.'

'There's nothing to forgive.' She sounded brittle. 'It

was entirely mutual. I'm not a teenager anymore and you gave me every chance to change my mind. You weren't to blame.'

It should have made him feel better. Instead he felt infinitely worse. 'But you regretted it afterwards,' he said harshly.

She ducked her head, then made an obvious effort to meet his eyes. 'That's not your fault.'

At a loss, he studied her face, seeing resolution and a hint of sadness, as if she were renouncing something she desperately wanted. He could almost feel her putting some emotional distance between them.

She said, 'If you took advantage, so did I. I used you.'

'*Used* me?' Shock roughened his voice.

'I wanted something…someone…to lean on. You were there.'

'I don't care! Lean on me anytime you like. I can stand it.'

'But I can't.'

'What do you mean by that?' Scowling, he said, 'Everyone needs support now and then.'

'Everyone?' She cast him a derisive look, and pulled her arm from his slackened grasp. 'If you let me know when the scaffolding's removed I'll finish the rest of the mosaic.'

He let her go, morosely watching her get into her car and drive away.

The next day, after closing the gallery and cashing up, Rhiannon went home.

When they'd had dinner, Janette switched on the television for a current affairs programme. Rhiannon, curled up in an armchair with a book in the hope that it would help her forget last night's events, paid little attention until the name Gerald Dodd burst on her ears like a gunshot.

Her head jerked up, and goose flesh rose on her arms as a smiling picture of the man flashed on the screen. Her feet shot to the floor, and she was ready to flee when the presenter said, '...denied allegations of a sexual nature concerning his patients. Tonight we interview the man who says he is the target of a woman scorned.'

Slowly Rhiannon sank back. Rage hammered at her forehead and hotly blocked her throat. She didn't hear the rest of the preliminaries before the interview, conducted in his consulting room.

It hadn't changed much. Neither had he. He spoke with pity of a deluded woman who had referred her friend to him with the specific agenda of having her back up a false accusation. He was charming, sorrowful and sympathetic, only lightly alluding to the fact that if the 'pathetic and ridiculous' allegations were believed the women might be in line for considerable monetary compensation. Rhiannon wondered how anyone could doubt his sincerity, or the compassion in his eyes.

'Do you believe him?' she asked Janette when the ad break came.

'He's convincing,' the other girl said. 'A bit too smooth, maybe. But he'll probably get off. It's their word against his, and they are friends, apparently. Difficult to prove it's not collusion.'

'He doesn't deserve to get off,' Rhiannon murmured. And then more fiercely, 'He doesn't!'

CHAPTER NINE

GABRIEL'S secretary left a message with Peri to say the scaffolding in the Angelair Building had been dismantled, leaving her no excuse not to continue with the mosaic.

On impulse she said, 'Peri, would you like to help me finish the Angelair project? I'll pay you, of course.'

'Yeah, okay,' he said. 'I'm no expert at mosaic but I've watched you often enough. I guess I could make myself useful.'

When Gabriel saw Peri at her side, working on the cartoon for the lower half of the mosaic, he cast her a piercing glance, lifting his brows derisively.

'Peri's going to help with the rest of the project,' she said, sending him a defiant look of her own.

'I see.' All too obviously, he did. He knew she was using Peri as a shield, taking the coward's way.

But that was better than laying herself open to perilous emotions that she didn't dare give way to again. Wasn't it?

Peri was an asset in more ways than one. With him to help carry tiles and materials she didn't need anyone else, and he quickly picked up her techniques. The work went amazingly fast, and when Gabriel came to watch them, for the most part he maintained a slightly brooding silence.

Once the mortaring and grouting was done, Rhiannon

said, 'I'll finish the rest myself.' There was still a little painting to be done, handwork that didn't need a second person. 'Thanks for your help, Peri.'

'Anytime.' He looked at her curiously. 'What's with you and the angel Gabriel?'

'Nothing. He likes to keep an eye on how his project's going.'

'Not only on that. He watches you like a hawk. Does he scare you?'

'Of course not.'

'Then why don't you ever look at him if you can help it? You're not going out with him any more, are you?'

'One show isn't "going out" with someone. Everything else was business.'

'Oh, yeah. You're running scared of *something*.' Peri scowled. 'If it's him, I'll sort him out for you.'

'Peri, no! He hasn't done anything to deserve that.'

Of course he hadn't. If she was running scared, it was from herself, her own unpredictable reactions and muddled emotions. It was time she sorted herself out. Maybe time to be brave enough to take a step in the dark.

She went back to the Angelair Building prepared to face Gabriel, to find only Mick, offering any help she might need. 'Mr Hudson told me to look after you while he's away,' he said.

'Gabriel's away?'

'Had to fly to Australia in a hurry. Didn't he tell you?'

'No.' There was no reason why he should, she supposed.

'His brother was in an accident over there,' Mick said. 'He's the manager of the Sydney office, you know.'

The memory of her parents' accident came back

sharply—the jolt of learning the news, then the black coldness of knowing her mother was dead, the mingled relief and fear when she was told her father was alive but in critical condition. And the continuing ache of his ongoing disability. 'How serious is it?'

'Dunno.' Mick shrugged. 'But Mr Hudson was worried.'

Gabriel hadn't spoken much of his family, but his tone when he mentioned his brother was affectionate. She wished he'd given her the chance to express her concern and sympathy. But his mind would have been preoccupied with his brother's needs, and making arrangements to go to him. Rhiannon had no right to expect him to think of contacting her.

Mick carried a stepladder to the landing for her, and stayed by her while she checked the mosaic over, making sure the tesserae were all firmly fixed, and donning a mask and gloves to clean a few bits that showed a leftover residue of grouting. The next evening she began adding silver paint in a broad swathe across part of the width, dividing it into two parts sweeping upward like abstract angel wings.

When she was done and Mick had removed the stepladder, she stood down in the foyer to survey the completed opus.

Mick came back. 'Pretty good,' he said. 'You'll be proud of yourself.'

Rhiannon smiled at him. It was exactly as she'd pictured, yet a tiny niggle of dissatisfaction bothered her.

But no amount of checking her drawings against the mosaic enlightened her as to what it was.

*   *   *

Peri found her poring over the picture of the Russian icon that had inspired her design, comparing it with her coloured plan.

'Something isn't right,' she said in answer to his query. 'But I can't figure it out.'

He joined her. 'It's a great design,' he said. 'Are you sure you're not just being over-perfectionist?'

Rhiannon shook her head. 'It feels unfinished. As if there's something missing.'

He looked from one piece of paper to the other with concentration. Finally he pointed to the picture of the angel and said hesitantly, 'Rhee…the only missing element apart from the halo around his head is the rose he's holding.'

Rhiannon stared at the flower in the angel's hand, instinctively recoiling. 'Oh, no!' she said aloud. 'It's an abstract! Not a copy.'

'Sure, but…' Peri shrugged uncomfortably. 'Well, it's up to you.'

The following evening Rhiannon entered the Angelair building. It had been blustery all morning, and a few showers had fallen. The swish of tyres through water added to the hum of traffic on the street and the roar of the digging machines next door. Lately the crews had been working until dark. Apparently the contractors were behind schedule.

Mick carried the stepladder up the stairs for her. 'I'll stick around while you're climbing up and down,' he said, testing it. 'There you go. She's steady.'

She had the picture of the Russian icon in one hand, and taped it to the mosaic, her mouth set in a stubborn line. Carefully she drew lines over the tesserae and the grouting, copying the rose stem and its single bloom as closely as she could, but making it much bigger. Gradually her tension eased as she concentrated on her meticulous brushstrokes.

Mick said, surprised, 'Even I can tell what that is!'

She smiled down at him. 'Can you pass me that paint?'

She painted in the stem and the leaves, and was dipping her brush for the final time into a pot of crimson when they heard the door from the side stairs open and close, and seconds later Gabriel appeared, looking up at them, Rhiannon perched near the top of the ladder that Mick was unnecessarily holding on to.

Gabriel's hair was wet, there were droplets of water on his face, and the shoulders of his jacket were damp. A low rumble of distant thunder vied with the city noise.

Rhiannon felt paralysed, the brush poised in her hand, as Gabriel swept his gaze over the mosaic, and then fixed on her. He said, 'I'll take over here, Mick.'

The older man looked up at Rhiannon for a second before starting down the stairs. 'How's your brother, Mr Hudson?' he asked.

Gabriel was still looking at Rhiannon, not moving at all. After a moment he shifted his glance and told Mick, 'He's not out of the woods yet but they say he's stable. Why don't you take the rest of the day off? I have a hell of a lot of paperwork to catch up on so I'll be around for a while.'

'Sure, boss. Ta. I wouldn't mind going out for a drink or two with a couple of old mates. They invited me but I said I was working tonight.'

After he'd left, Gabriel finally moved, slowly ascending the stairs. He looked tired and stressed, his cheeks slightly hollowed, the skin of his face taut. He stopped at the foot of the ladder. 'I didn't know if you'd be here,' he said. 'I thought maybe this would be finished.'

'I'm so sorry about your brother. Mick told me there'd been an accident.'

'Some drunk smashed into his car. The doctors had to remove his spleen and patch him up in various ways. He broke a few bones too but we hope he's going to pull through. His wife is with him, and my mother. I'm not needed any more.'

You are, Rhiannon thought. *I need you.* The thought was so terrifying it paralysed her.

He shifted his gaze to what she'd been doing. 'Don't let me disturb you. Watching you work is…soothing.'

'I'm nearly finished.' She lifted the paintbrush, making a careful curve at the edge of a petal.

A few more strokes and it was done. She refastened the lid on the tin, laid the brush on top and handed them down to Gabriel. 'Can you take this?'

He placed them on the drop sheet, then as she climbed down steadied the ladder with both hands, so that when she turned she was within his extended arms.

Her heart flipped over, but she looked up at him fearlessly, meeting his questioning gaze. Slowly she raised a hand and placed it against his chest, letting it lie there.

He leaned forward, tilting his head, giving her time to draw away, but she didn't.

His lips were cool from the rain that she smelled on him, but they warmed when he found her mouth with a kiss that was sure and slow, redolent of restrained eroticism. She closed her eyes and savoured it, every atom of concentration on the firm masculine mouth that was parting hers, gently insistent.

Then he drew away. 'I hope you don't mind,' he said, his voice deep and slightly gritty. 'I needed that.'

'So did I,' she said, and as a flame leapt into his eyes she slid her arms about his neck and offered her mouth to him again.

His hands left the ladder and his arms came about her waist, hauling her close. But he paused, consciously loosening his hold, and Rhiannon gave a little choking cry and tiptoed to meet his kiss. He was being so careful of her, so considerate. Her heart melted like metal in a furnace and she opened her mouth to him, inviting him, trusting him, wanting him…

She had a sensation of soaring far above the ground, caught in some kind of celestial wind. It was Gabriel who broke the kiss, pressing his lips to her cheek, and then to the curve of her shoulder and neck.

He kissed her mouth again, quick and urgent. He looked upward, his eyes lighting on the surreal face of the angel she'd fashioned. 'Thank you,' he breathed.

His expression changed as his gaze shifted to the recently applied paint that glistened in the fierce white glow of the lamps. 'That rose wasn't in the original design.'

'No. Do you mind?'

He shook his head, and looked back at her, his eyes ablaze with curiosity and something else. 'I like it. Why did you do it?'

'It belongs. I don't know why, but it seems right.'

'Yes,' he said, glancing again at the mosaic. 'Have you signed it?'

'No.' She hadn't wanted to until she had resolved that nagging doubt about its completion. She crouched to scrawl her painted initials in one corner, and then joined him at the top of the stairs.

He said, 'Congratulations. It's a great asset to the building. People will be talking about it.'

'It's probably the best thing I've done, as well as the biggest. Thank you for giving me the chance.' She looked down at the brush she still held. 'I suppose we ought to clear all this stuff away. And I should clean my brushes.'

If he'd said, Don't bother, she'd have followed his lead. But he merely nodded and began packing up the lights. She remembered he'd said he had a lot of work to do after his absence.

Gabriel locked the storeroom door and handed Rhiannon the key. 'There are a couple of things I really do have to attend to urgently,' he said. 'Is it too much to ask you to come up to my office and wait for me? I want to talk to you, be with you.'

She wanted that, too. 'I'd like that.'

Pausing beside the elevators, Gabriel said, 'We'll take the stairs…'

'No, it's all right.' When the doors opened she hesitated a second before stepping into the small, brightly lit space, and Gabriel pressed the button for his office floor.

The doors closed and the car began to rise, all sound from outside suddenly cut off. Rhiannon was standing a few feet away from him, her back to the wall, and he recalled the first time he'd seen her, retreating from him into a corner of an elevator similar to this one.

Then a muffled bang came from somewhere outside, the elevator jerked to a dead stop and the light went out.

Gabriel let fly a single swearword. He fumbled his hand over the control panel, pressed a couple of buttons without much hope.

Nothing happened.

Rhiannon hadn't made a sound. He couldn't see a thing in the thick, stuffy blackness. 'Rhiannon? Are you okay?'

'Yes.' But he could hear the strain in the single syllable.

'It's all right,' he said. 'Just a power cut.' In the dark he located the emergency phone and lifted it, his heart sinking at the deafening silence on the other end. Futilely he shook it.

He tried to prise the doors apart without success, and muttered, 'Damn!'

'What?' Rhiannon asked.

Trying to sound reassuring, he said, 'We're not in any danger, but the emergency phone isn't working. We do have an occasional problem with vandalism, but at a guess, more likely one of the diggers on the next door excavation cut through some cables and knocked out both the phone and power lines.'

'Your cell phone…' she suggested tightly. 'I don't have mine.'

'It won't work in here.'

Cursing the darkness, he began moving slowly towards her. 'We're stuck for now, but hopefully it won't be long before it's fixed.' Mick had left the building some time ago and if he stayed out late it could be hours before anyone realised their predicament. Even then he might not know they were still here.

His hand touched cool skin—her arm. She drew in a breath and pulled away.

'It's me,' he said foolishly. Who else would she think it was?

'I know.' Her voice was tight and cold. 'Don't touch me. Please.'

Gabriel suffered a wave of shock, a kind of outrage. He was already rattled, his equilibrium seriously out of whack. Trapped and helpless—which wasn't a condition he relished—with a woman he knew was deathly afraid of exactly this situation, and he was unable to see any way of getting her out of it.

And now Rhiannon was acting as if she expected him to attack her.

'For God's sake!' he snarled. 'When have I ever given you reason to be afraid of me?'

A great way to gain her confidence, he realised bleakly, but his patience had snapped, driving him on. 'What the hell happened to you anyway?'

She didn't answer, and he pummelled the wall with a fist, pushed at the unmoving doors. He swore again, loudly, uncaring if he shocked Rhiannon.

She said, her voice coming from the darkness behind him, 'I'm sorry.'

'For what?' The apology didn't mollify him. If anyone should be apologising, it was him, but knowing that only made him angrier.

'I'm not afraid of you, Gabriel.' He heard a faint rustle of movement, but couldn't see a thing. 'I was afraid that if you…if you held me, I'd have hysterics all over you. And that wouldn't do either of us any good.'

Oh, God. She was holding herself together by the merest thread. That was the reason for the clipped, controlled speech, the refusal to accept physical support. She was fighting terror but determined not to give in to it, fighting it alone in her own damnably independent fashion. And he'd yelled at her.

'Feel free,' he said. 'You're welcome to have hysterics for both of us.' And was relieved when he heard a shaky, smothered laugh.

'Are you scared?' she asked.

'Not scared. Annoyed that I can't get you out of this. You really hate it, don't you?'

'Not as much as I would have if I'd been alone.'

Well, that was hopeful. 'It might be a while before we get out of here,' he said carefully. 'So we may as well make ourselves as comfortable as we can. Are you cold?'

'No, it's quite muggy, actually.'

'Let me know if you want to borrow my jacket.'

'Thanks.'

His eyes were beginning to adjust. He could just make out her slightly paler form against the prevailing blackness as she slid to the floor against the far wall, a huddled shape.

Gabriel followed suit, folding his arms and leaning his head against the nearest wall, letting his long legs stretch in front of him, careful to keep them away from her. Wishing she'd let him come near.

He ached to fold her into his arms and protect her,

comfort her. Only she didn't want him to. And he had to respect that.

He tried hard to see her, frustrated by the heavy blackness that pressed upon them. He thought she was hugging her knees, perhaps literally holding herself together.

Casting about in his mind for a topic of conversation that might distract her from their predicament, he found nothing but a yawning blank. All coherent thought seemed to have deserted him.

Then into the darkness she said, 'I'm going to give evidence against Doctor Dodd.'

Jolted, he said, 'You are?'

'I went to the police and told them…everything. You were right, I have to do it.'

Gabriel swallowed. That must have been hellishly difficult. And he hadn't been here. 'When is the case?'

'Next week.'

'I'll come with you.'

'No.'

Something in his chest ached, tightly. 'Do you have someone?'

'I have to do this on my own.'

'Why?'

She was quiet for a long time, so that he thought she wasn't going to answer. When she did speak, it didn't seem to have anything to do with the question.

Into the darkness, she said, 'Five years ago, I was kidnapped.'

Of all the possibilities he had imagined, that one hadn't entered his mind. *'Kidnapped?'* He had to do some radical adjustment to his thinking. From what she'd said, he didn't think her family had been wealthy. 'Was it a hostage situation?'

'No.' She was silent for so long he thought she wasn't going to say any more, but apparently she'd been gathering her thoughts. At last she said, 'I knew him, from one of my classes at university. He asked me out a couple of times, and he was quite nice, but the third time I turned him down.'

She paused again and Gabriel dared to ask, 'Why?'

'He was so intense…it made me uncomfortable. He told me he'd watched me for ages before plucking up the nerve to ask me out. And he said such extravagant things…about how he'd waited for me all his life, and how he'd never look at another woman. At first I laughed, but he got offended. I was a late starter in one-on-one relationships, concentrated on my studies all through school, and it was my first uni year. I couldn't cope with that kind of…obsession.'

'So you broke it off. The sensible thing to do.'

'Yes. Then I lost my mother, and he was so sympathetic—kind, very helpful. He'd lost his when he was a kid, and he seemed to understand. Somehow…we drifted into a sort of girlfriend/boyfriend relationship.'

'And then…?' Gabriel prompted quietly.

'He became gradually more and more possessive. I couldn't go anywhere, see anyone—even my girl-friends—without him checking up on me. It wasn't healthy, and in the end I couldn't stand it. But he wouldn't get out of my life. He began sending me long, rambling love letters, and flowers—huge, expensive bouquets. Almost every day. He'd hang around after my classes, until one day I yelled at him to leave me alone.

He phoned that night and told me off for speaking to him like that in front of other people, but he didn't approach me again, and the flowers stopped. He'd loiter at a distance and watch, instead. Then the silent phone calls began. I knew it was him, but he never spoke.'

'Did you go to the police?'

'I didn't think that was warranted. He'd never threatened me in any way, and I thought if I kept ignoring him he'd give up.'

'But he didn't.'

'After a lecture one night he stopped me. He said he realised he'd been stupid, apologised for embarrassing me, and told me he'd like to explain. I said there was no need, but I let him persuade me to have a coffee with him, I suppose because I felt a bit guilty and sorry for him, and he said first he'd got to get his jacket from his car. I walked there with him. He'd parked under a tree, and he opened the luggage compartment and fished around with one hand, then asked me to hold up the lid because the hinge was broken. The next thing I knew he'd shoved me in there and locked it. It was so quick— he had it all planned. There were people about, but I don't think anyone saw a thing. I didn't even have time to scream.'

Gabriel felt every muscle tighten. She was reciting all this with determined calm, her voice so flat it was almost emotionless. But she must have been petrified. 'Where did he take you?'

'He had this place out in the bush, though I had no idea where we were when he finally let me out and hustled me into it—an old house, no neighbours. At one time it was a farmhouse, but the land around had reverted to trees and scrub, and no one had lived there for ages. He said we were meant for each other and we needed time together.'

Gabriel started to speak, and found there was an obstruction in his throat. 'How long did he keep you there?'

'Six days. It's not long really, but it seemed a lifetime.'

'It must have.' She wouldn't have known how long it would last, or what the man was likely to do to her.

'The first night, neither of us slept. He didn't…molest me, just kept saying over and over that we belonged together and that this was a time-out to give me a chance to realise it, without distractions. I tried to reason with him, argued, pleaded, shouted, threatened him with the police. Told him he had to take me home, or at least back to the city somewhere, promised I wouldn't tell anyone. He just went on being patient.'

'Patient!' Gabriel exploded.

'Never raised his voice. But then I said I had to go to the toilet and I took the louvres out of the window and got out. He came after me and…'

Gabriel's skin crawled. 'What?'

'There was a shipping container at the back of the house. I suppose someone had brought it in to use as a storage shed or something. It had a padlock.'

'He *locked you in?*'

'He kept on going in to university. Every day he left me—with food and drink, a mattress…and a bucket. It was hot in the daytime, but there were overhanging trees so it didn't get direct sun. He'd bored tiny airholes in the sides. He told me it was just until I came to my senses and realised we were meant to be together. But it was dark, except for the little bit of light that came in through those holes. And so small.'

About the size of an elevator, Gabriel thought, swallowing.

'He brought me roses,' she said, hushed. 'Red roses. Every day. I've never forgotten the scent. He'd make dinner and then take me into the house, and we'd have a meal together, with a fresh bouquet of roses on the table. It was bizarre.'

That was putting it mildly. 'It was sick!'

'He was sick. He's in a secure mental facility now.'

The best place for him, Gabriel thought. And the safest. Sick or not, if Gabriel ever ran up against him he'd have trouble keeping himself from smashing the guy's face.

'He never took his eyes off me until he needed to sleep. Then he'd…politely ask me to go to bed with him, and when I said no, he'd shake his head sadly and take me back to the container. One night I actually said yes, hoping to catch him off guard somehow and take his car keys, get away. I was even prepared to have sex with him, wait for him to go to sleep before I sneaked out, but then, what if he just locked me up again afterwards? And when we were in bed, I found I couldn't go through with it anyway, and fought him off. That was the only time he was angry. He dragged me back to the container naked, and…the next day he didn't leave me any food.'

Gabriel uncurled his fingers, flexing them. He had to fight a renewed wave of nausea. 'How did you get away?'

'My grandmother had reported me missing, and my

friends told the police what had been going on. Thank God they took it seriously. They questioned him, and later followed him when he left the university. They were watching when he unlocked the container, but…'

The silence almost breathed. Gabriel stirred, containing his instinct to go to her. 'What then?'

'They were armed. He had a knife. He said he'd kill us both if they tried to take me from him. He meant it,' she added starkly. 'They didn't dare to approach him. He pulled us both into the container and closed the door. We were in there for hours, while he kept watch from the air holes.'

Gabriel closed his eyes, squeezing them shut. He unclamped tight lips. 'No wonder you don't like confined spaces.'

'Not my favourite thing,' she agreed huskily. 'By that time he was beyond reason. In the end I lied to him, said I realised now he really loved me, and he'd persuaded me we did belong together for all eternity. Everything he'd said. I said I wanted to marry him, there and then. Told him if we were married I couldn't testify against him and the police couldn't hold him, so we…could still be together.'

'That isn't true anymore, is it?'

'I don't think so, but he accepted it. I suppose because he wanted to believe I…loved him. He asked for a minister. They said they'd get one, and sent in a policeman wearing a dog-collar.'

Gabriel let out a breath. 'You weren't hurt?'

'No. They grabbed him and it was all over.'

Except for the trauma she'd suffered. Post-traumatic

stress, they called it. She must have had a doozy of a dose.

'That's why you needed counselling,' he said.

'Yes. And Doctor Dodd helped me a lot, at first. I was in such a mess I couldn't even walk down the street alone. Getting into an elevator was impossible. I slept with the light on for months. Being alone with a man— even a doctor—freaked me out. My grandmother came to all my appointments until I trusted him enough to do without her.'

Rhiannon paused, and Gabriel said harshly, 'And then he betrayed you.'

'I'd been seeing him for months. He was my lifeline to sanity and normality. He began by just holding my hand, saying I needed to get used to normal touching. It made sense. Then he'd stroke my hands, my arms, my hair, my neck. I didn't like it but he was so persuasive... I thought I had to get used to it, that it was a necessary part of my therapy.'

Gabriel muttered a forceful word under his breath.

'When he touched me in other places, I could scarcely believe what he was doing. When I challenged him he said I was suffering from sex-based trauma—frigidity— and with my consent to treatment he could help me. Fortunately I had enough sense to recognise his arguments for what they were. I knew what he was doing was wrong.'

'Even if you had consented, it would still be rape.'

'I know. But you see...'

'You decided not to trust anyone, not to ask anyone for support or help, because you were afraid they'd let you down.'

'Something like that,' she agreed, her voice a whisper.

'You trusted your grandmother.'

'Of course I did!'

'But she died—left you.'

'She couldn't help it!'

'Your mother died, too—and your father can't be a father to you anymore.'

'What are you trying to say?'

'You won't allow yourself to depend on anyone. It wasn't only Dodd—everyone you depended on abandoned you, one way or another.'

'They didn't abandon me! I wasn't a child!'

'You were seventeen—not an adult. You're afraid to lean on anyone—that's why you won't let me get close. While my brother's wife and I were sitting by his bedside, I did as much leaning as she did, Rhiannon. We supported each other, and when my mother came we all cried in each other's arms.'

'You're family. I don't have a family anymore. It's not the same. I can't expect that of anyone.'

'You could. I love you, Rhiannon. I want to marry you, and live happily ever after with you. I can't promise not to die, but as long as I live, I want to be the person you give your support to, the way you did tonight when I came up the stairs to you and you understood without words, gave me what I needed. And the person who supports you when you need it.'

She didn't speak for so long he couldn't hold his tongue any longer. 'Rhiannon?'

After a little pause she said, 'You know what? I am cold now.'

'Come here,' he said, slipping off his jacket.

It was a moment before he discerned the faint blur of movement. Then the shadows stirred, and she was beside him, the scent of her rising subtly to his nostrils. He arranged the jacket like a blanket over her shoulders, slid an arm about her and pulled her closer to him, his arms loosely cradling her as she nestled against his chest.

'Won't you be cold?' she asked doubtfully.

'Not as long as you stay right here,' he answered.

Right here where she belonged.

CHAPTER TEN

RHIANNON was suddenly very tired. Gabriel's body was warm at her back, his arms wrapped around her. Despite being trapped in a situation that had brought back her worst nightmares, she felt safe now. Secure.

'I love you, Gabriel,' she said, and felt his arms tighten, his breath stop. 'I've been in love with you for ages, but I wasn't brave enough—or whole enough—to take that step in the dark. I was so afraid that if I loved you and you left me, I'd be right back where I'd been after…all that happened years ago. I wanted to love you as you deserve to be loved, as I deserve to love. Like a strong, free woman—a woman who doesn't need a prop or a guardian angel. That's what gave me the courage to go to the police about Gerald Dodd. I know it will break my heart if you leave me, that life will never be as perfect again, but I'll survive even that.'

'I'll never leave you,' he told her huskily, his cheek against her hair. 'Never voluntarily. Wherever I am, even if I die, I'll be with you always, I swear.'

He shifted their position so that he could reach her mouth, and seal it with a long, sweet kiss. 'You haven't said yes,' he reminded her. 'Will you marry me?'

'Yes,' she said. 'Just as soon as we get out of this damned lift.'

* * *

Rhiannon was dozing against Gabriel's shoulder when the light flickered on and the elevator began to move. It stopped as if nothing had ever gone wrong, and the doors slid open to reveal Mick, wearing baggy sweats instead of his uniform, and an anxious expression. 'You okay?' he queried them as they scrambled to their feet. 'Some dumb ass cut through the cables.'

Gabriel tucked his arm about Rhiannon and they stepped onto the carpeted floor. 'I've never been so okay in my life.'

'Ah-huh!' Mick said slowly, looking from him to Rhiannon, and began to grin.

'I don't suppose you happen to have a marriage celebrant's licence?' Gabriel asked.

Mick's grin grew. ''Fraid not, boss. You're getting married?'

'She promised,' Gabriel told him, 'as soon as we got out of that damned lift. But I guess we'll have to wait a while.'

But not for long. Gabriel was on hot bricks until the day that Rhiannon promised to love, honour and cherish him for the rest of her days, after he'd promised the same to her. Mick had proudly led her down the aisle to his side, and from the time she put her hand in Gabriel's and he slipped his ring onto her finger, he hardly let it go.

They left the reception by taxi, on their way to one of Auckland's top hotels for the night. Across his knees, Gabriel held a long, narrow white box. At the front door of the Angelair Building he told the driver to stop and wait for them, mystifying Rhiannon.

'I want to give thanks to my namesake,' he said, leading Rhiannon up the stairs. He paused before the mosaic, its colours gleaming softly in the light from the chandeliers. 'That rose,' he said, looking up at it. 'Did it upset you to paint it?'

'It was sort of cathartic in a way. I didn't want to do it, but I knew I had to. Once it was there, it was just a rose, and a sort of symbol of all that I've achieved…conquered.'

'Then,' Gabriel said, 'I hope you won't mind this.' He opened the box and lifted out a single, long-stemmed red rose, and laid it reverently at the foot of the mosaic, then stepped back, taking her hand.

'I don't mind,' she said. 'It's a lovely gesture.'

'One day,' he said, 'I'd like to be able to give you flowers.' Today she'd carried a mother-of-pearl prayer book that had been her grandmother's, not flowers.

'One day,' she said, 'I'll like that, if they come from you.'

He bent to kiss her, and she kissed him back with eagerness, until he broke away. 'We have a taxi waiting,' he said hoarsely, 'a honeymoon suite, and a bed.' He turned to the mosaic and sketched a small salute. 'Goodnight, Gabe. Sorry, but you aren't invited. This is not angel stuff.'

Then he swept Rhiannon, laughing, into his arms and carried her down the stairs to the waiting taxi.

'Where to now?' the driver asked, after Gabriel had shut the doors of the building and rejoined his still smiling wife.

Gabriel looked at Rhiannon, took her hand firmly in his and said, 'Heaven.'

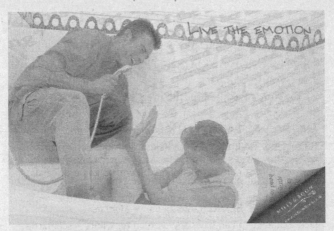

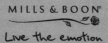

MILLS & BOON®

Live the emotion

Modern Romance™

MISTRESS FOR A MONTH *by Miranda Lee*

Rico Mandretti knows Renée Selensky despises him, and her history makes her as potent as poison. Then Fate delivers Rico an unbeatable hand: he wins a game of cards – and Renée into the bargain!

IN SEPARATE BEDROOMS *by Carole Mortimer*

Jack Beauchamp can have any woman he wants – so Mattie Crawford can't understand why he's so determined to take *her* to Paris. Maybe a weekend in the French capital with the best-looking, most charming man she's ever met is his idea of a punishment…

THE ITALIAN'S LOVE-CHILD *by Sharon Kendrick*

Millionaire Luca Cardelli broke Eve's heart years ago, and now he's back. Eve is soon entrapped in the whirlwind of their love affair but her shock is only equalled by Luca's outrageous reaction to some surprising news…

THE GREEK'S VIRGIN BRIDE *by Julia James*

When Andrea Fraser is unexpectedly summoned to Greece she is shocked at the news that awaits her. Her grandfather has found her a husband! Nikos Vassilis may be the most sophisticated man she's ever encountered, but she'll be leaving at the first opportunity – won't she…?

On sale 3rd October 2003

Available at most branches of WHSmith, Tesco, Martins, Borders, Eason, Sainsbury's and all good paperback bookshops.

0903/01a

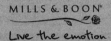

MILLS & BOON®

Live the emotion

Modern Romance™

THE BILLIONAIRE'S CONTRACT BRIDE *by Carol Marinelli*

Zavier Chambers is one of Australia's most powerful playboys, and to him Tabitha appears to be the worst kind of woman. Tabitha isn't a gold-digger – but she does need to marry for money. When Zavier blackmails her into marriage she has no choice…

THE TYCOON'S TROPHY MISTRESS *by Lee Wilkinson*

Daniel Wolfe is not a man to be messed with – and he already has an agenda of his own. Charlotte Michaels soon finds herself being offered an unexpected career move – as her boss's mistress!

THE MARRIAGE RENEWAL *by Maggie Cox*

When Tara's husband returns after five years, she is willing to give him his divorce – but not until she has told Mac about what happened after he left. Mac is stunned, but he's as consumed with desire for her as he ever was. Is their passion a strong enough basis on which to renew their marriage vows?

MARRIED TO A MARINE *by Cathie Linz*

Justice Wilder was badly injured while saving a child's life – and now may be facing the end of his military career. Kelly Hart tracks him down in order to convince him to accept help for the first time in his life. But what happens when he discovers she used to love him…?

On sale 3rd October 2003

Available at most branches of WHSmith, Tesco, Martins, Borders, Eason, Sainsbury's and all good paperback bookshops.

0903/01b

FREE
4 BOOKS
AND A SURPRISE GIFT!

We would like to take this opportunity to thank you for reading this Mills & Boon® book by offering you the chance to take FOUR more specially selected titles from the Modern Romance™ series absolutely FREE! We're also making this offer to introduce you to the benefits of the Reader Service™—

- ★ FREE home delivery
- ★ FREE monthly Newsletter
- ★ FREE gifts and competitions
- ★ Exclusive Reader Service discount
- ★ Books available before they're in the shops

Accepting these FREE books and gift places you under no obligation to buy; you may cancel at any time, even after receiving your free shipment. Simply complete your details below and return the entire page to the address below. *You don't even need a stamp!*

YES! Please send me 4 free Modern Romance™ books and a surprise gift. I understand that unless you hear from me, I will receive 6 superb new titles every month for just £2.60 each, postage and packing free. I am under no obligation to purchase any books and may cancel my subscription at any time. The free books and gift will be mine to keep in any case.

P3ZED

Ms/Mrs/Miss/Mr ....Initials ....
BLOCK CAPITALS PLEASE

Surname ....

Address ....

....

....Postcode ....

Send this whole page to:
UK: FREEPOST CN81, Croydon, CR9 3WZ
EIRE: PO Box 4546, Kilcock, County Kildare (stamp required)